Maisie Morris and the Whopping Lies

Joanna Nadin is the author of *Maisie Morris and the Awful Arkwrights* and *Solomon Smee Versus the Monkeys*. *Maisie Morris and the Whopping Lies* is her third book and was inspired by her younger brother James. Joanna says, "He told the most fantastical fibs as a child. For example, 'Bunny took me to Egypt last night and we ate a crocodile.' He grew up to be a journalist. So I imagined an evil version of James and then sent Maisie Morris and Monkey Onassis out to get him!" Joanna's previous jobs include working as a lifeguard, radio newsreader, wardrobe assistant – during which she washed the underpants of many famous people – and adviser to the Prime Minister. She is now a political writer and editor. Joanna lives in Bath.

By the same author

Maisie Morris and the Awful Arkwrights
Solomon Smee Versus the Monkeys

Maisie Morris
and the
Whopping Lies

Joanna Nadin

illustrated by Arthur Robins

WALKER BOOKS
AND SUBSIDIARIES

LONDON · BOSTON · SYDNEY · AUCKLAND

First published 2005 by Walker Books Ltd
87 Vauxhall Walk, London SE11 5HJ

2 4 6 8 10 9 7 5 3 1

Text © 2005 Joanna Nadin
Illustrations © 2005 Arthur Robins

The right of Joanna Nadin and Arthur Robins to be identified
as author and illustrator respectively of this work has been
asserted by them in accordance with the Copyright,
Designs and Patents Act 1988

This book has been typeset in Randumhouse and Shinn Light

Printed in Great Britain by Cox & Wyman Ltd, Reading, Berkshire

British Library Cataloguing in Publication Data:
a catalogue record for this book
is available from the British Library

ISBN 1-84428-950-8

www.walkerbooks.co.uk

For Amelia, who was born halfway down page 73

Lies

Have you ever told a lie?

Maybe it was just a small fib like: "Why no, Great-aunt Augusta, I can hardly see your moustache at all." When in fact her upper lip is as hairy as a mammoth's armpit.

Or maybe it was a whopper like: "No, I did not bite my little sister Amelia; a giant dog called Rex snuck in the window and did it – I saw him."

The trouble with the whopping sort is that they cause all manner of bother and hot water. So if you ever feel one boiling up inside you, itching to get out, zip your mouth up quick and swallow hard!

Some people, however, never learn to zip up. Lester Sylvester was one of them.

Lester Sylvester

In the bottom right-hand corner of England sat a very small and very dull town called Groutley, home of the not-so-famous Hosepipe Museum, and Peabody and Nidgett's department store, which only stocked extra-large tweed suits and doilies.

In the middle of Groutley High Street, just past Fishcoteque takeaway and Totally Trousers men's outfitters, and immediately before the turning into the Bernard Gibbons Memorial Multi-Storey Car Park, sat the offices of the *Groutley Chronicle*.

And inside those modern, concrete offices, behind a glass door with EDITOR on it in large black capitals, sat Lester Sylvester.

Lester Sylvester was a sweaty sort of man, with bad teeth and fat arms like joints of ham. He wore his shirtsleeves rolled up and always had a pencil behind his ear, and a nasty thin cigarette hanging out of his mouth.

Lester told lies. Not just little fibs, but big hairy whoppers.

When he was small, he lied to his mother.

"Stop picking your nose, Lester," she would say.

"I'm not," he would reply, one finger firmly wedged up his left nostril. "I'm communicating with aliens."

When he started school, he lied to his teachers.

"What pets do you have, Lester?" asked Miss Bunnet one morning.

"I have a werewolf called Horace who lives in my airing cupboard," said Lester.

When he was older, Lester lied to his friends.

"I once climbed Everest in nothing but a kagoule," he told them.

And when he was a young man, he lied to the ladies.

"I am the heir to the throne of a small kingdom in Outer Perratootoo," he said at the disco.

No matter how hard he tried, Lester could not stop lying. Which is why he loved being the editor of a newspaper. He got paid to lie.

If a small boy had stolen a packet of strawberry

shoelaces from Mr Majoob's kiosk, Lester's report would say *"Marauding gangs of sweet-toothed thieves have plundered Groutley's top confectionery outlet."*

And if an old lady had twisted her ankle on a tricky paving slab, Lester's headline would proclaim *"Pensioner in Perilous Pavement Plunder – council to be sued for millions."*

He was such a fibber that the *Groutley Chronicle's* motto, printed in red on the front page of every edition, was not "Truth Above All" or "Truth, the Whole Truth and Nothing But the Truth" or some other admirable aim. It was "Who Dares Wins". Which was actually the motto for the SAS, an extremely dangerous and heroic organization and as unlike the *Groutley Chronicle* as chalk is cheese.

But the trouble with Groutley was that nothing exciting ever happened, so Lester's fibs had to stay small or someone might notice what he was up to.

One morning he picked up the *Chronicle* and read the stories out loud to himself.

"New clues in dog dropping mystery – an exclusive interview with council clear-up man Reg Yonkers," he read.

"Disco inferno at Razzmatazz Roller Rink over-60s' night!" he continued. "Silver skater Alf Dubbs falls asleep while smoking his pipe at rinkside café Meals on Wheels, mildly singeing his tank top and a gingham tablecloth."

Lester slammed the paper down on his desk. "Boring, boring and double boring with knobs on."

What Lester really dreamed of was a gruesome murder or a kidnapping.

"Imagine that on the front page of my paper," he said to himself, wringing his sweaty hands with anticipation. "Something to really shake Groutley up. Maybe a little old lady or a small child taken away by mysterious thugs in the night. Now that," he said, "would send my sales figures rocketing."

12

But as I have told you, Groutley is a small and dull town, and nothing as vile as that would ever happen. Would it?

Maisie Morris

On the outskirts of Groutley, behind a pair of old iron gates and at the end of a long and slightly overgrown gravelly drive, sat the large and creaky-looking Withering Heights Retirement Home.

On one side of Withering Heights, leaning off at a slight angle, sat a small and very spindly turret. And 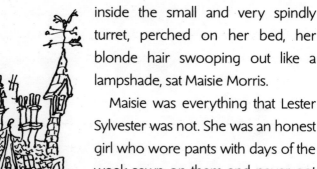 inside the small and very spindly turret, perched on her bed, her blonde hair swooping out like a lampshade, sat Maisie Morris.

Maisie was everything that Lester Sylvester was not. She was an honest girl who wore pants with days of the week sewn on them and never got the day wrong, she was the thrice winner of St Regina's Primary School prize for macramé owls, she loved animals and old people, always ate her greens and, most importantly, she never, ever told lies.

You may think that makes her sound rather boring. In which case I will assume you have never read of how Maisie's mother, Marigold, single-handedly scrubbed and polished Withering Heights and all its elderly residents from top to bottom every day as well as getting Maisie ready for school. Or how they all lived in fear of Withering Heights' odious owners, the Awful Arkwrights, who served cabbage water for lunch, confiscated pets and cancelled Christmas. Or how a travelling magician helped Maisie thwart the Arkwrights and left her ma in charge of the residents, and Maisie in charge of a small brown monkey called Monkey Onassis, who happened to be a former international jewel thief.

So you see, you couldn't be further from the truth.

But right then, Maisie was not doing anything even vaguely heroic. She was spending the very last day of her summer holidays deeply engrossed in the latest copy of *Monkeys Galore* magazine, trying in vain to identify what sort of monkey Monkey Onassis was, so that she'd know how to teach him to behave.

Monkey Onassis, on the other hand, was deeply engrossed in removing the feathers from one of the pillows on Maisie's bed and scattering them on the floor so that it looked as if it had been snowing.

"Baboon?" read Maisie. "Crested Gibbon? Devil-handed Howler? Owl-faced? Snub-nosed? Moustached or Woolly?"

Maisie sighed and looked at Monkey Onassis, who was a dull brown colour with no moustache, owl-face, snub-nose or any other interesting features. Or at least he was most days of the week – at that moment was covered in white feathers.

"No, I don't think you sound like any of those."

"Hoop!" said Monkey Onassis and pushed a handful of feathers underneath the duvet.

Maisie smiled. She loved Monkey Onassis more than anyone in the world (except her ma, of course). More than Colonel Snell, who had once been in charge of the King George VIII Royal Emergency Gardening Battalion. More than Loveday Pink, who wore exotic headdresses and taught her to dance the fandango. And even more than the new guest Ramsey McDoon, who at that very moment was

sitting next to Maisie on a wooden chair in the small and very spindly turret, reading that morning's *Groutley Chronicle.*

Ramsey had arrived in Groutley three weeks ago with a large tartan suitcase, a wild, whiskery ginger beard and a smile wider than the Firth of Forth. Maisie had liked him instantly. He told her wonderful tales of his days as Chief of Police on the Kyle of Tongue and of all the crooks he had nearly caught and mysteries he had nearly solved.

Some of his tales sounded a little tall to Maisie but she didn't mind because they were always fun.

Ramsey had retired from the police over twenty years ago with an ingrowing toenail. When Maisie asked him why he'd come to Groutley, he said he'd stuck a pin in a map. First of all it had hit somewhere called Saffron Walden – which, he said, sounded too strange. Then it had hit Hull – which, he said, smelled of cat food. Finally it had hit Groutley – which, he thought, sounded interesting. Although he was beginning to change his mind.

18

"What a tiresome wee town this is," protested Ramsey as he slapped the newspaper down on his lap, causing feathers to whirl around the room. "Not a single mysterious going-on."

Maisie peered up from an article on Needle-Nailed Night Monkeys.

"What sort of mysterious going-on are you looking for?" she asked.

"Och, I don't rightly know," Ramsey said, frowning and stroking his ginger beard. "Something a little different that I can get my teeth into and solve. A fearsome beastie, like a vampire maybe or a nice hound of hell."

Maisie's eyes widened. "Did you get many fearsome beasties on the Kyle of Tongue?" she asked.

"Och aye!" said Ramsey, smiling at the memory. "Did I never tell you about the time I nearly caught the mysterious shrieking Boggart of Bogle?"

"Yes," laughed Maisie. "But it turned out to be Bridie McGhee's bagpipes!"

"Aye," said Ramsey. "That it did."

"I don't think we get boggarts or vampires in Groutley," Maisie said. "There might be some bats in

19

the Scout hut roof. And Ma swears there's gremlins in the tumble-dryer. Is that any good?"

"Och no, lassie. But thanks anyway," said Ramsey.

"Nothing mysterious ever happens here," said Maisie with a sigh. "Not since Gaston Cummerbund left anyway."

"Aye, lass." Ramsey nodded. "I'd like to have met your magician fellow. He sounds like a grand chap."

"He was," said Maisie sadly.

"Och, don't be upset," said Ramsey and he ruffled her hair so that it swooped out even more. "At least you've got me! And Monkey Onassis, of course!"

Maisie looked at Monkey Onassis, who had finished unstuffing the pillow and was starting to unpick the multicoloured patchwork pieces of the quilt.

He was super. Maisie liked the way he hooped loudly in her ear to wake her up in the morning. She liked the way he hung around her neck to save himself walking anywhere. And most of all she liked the fact that he liked her just as much as she liked him.

Mrs Morris, on the other hand, was not so enamoured of Monkey Onassis, largely on account of the mess he left in his wake.

So far that summer he had unscrewed the handle from Mr Nidgett's bathroom door so that he was stuck in the toilet for several hours. He had pushed a banana inside the Hoover tube, causing it to backfire in an enormous cloud of dust and yellow mash all over the rumpus room beetle drive. And he had eaten, drunk, broken, dismantled or otherwise ruined, two kettles, a raffia rug, Maisie's tricycle, four bags of geranium scented bath salts and a bottle of Scourfield's All Purpose Super Strength Cleaning Fluid – good for blackened broiling pans, oily engines and headlice.

So his latest efforts with the pillow did not best please Mrs Morris when she came to find Maisie for tea.

"Crikey be, Maisie Morris!" she said, blowing fluff out of her face and waving her arms frantically. "I feel like I'm stuck in one of those souvenir snowstorm things you put on your mantelpiece – only without the reindeer or the model of Blackpool Tower."

"Sorry, Ma," said Maisie.

"Lawks, I know how much you love that creature," continued Mrs Morris, "but if he destroys any more soft furnishings, he'll have to stay in his biscuit tin until he learns his lesson."

"Och, don't do that, Mrs Morris," said Ramsey. "The poor wee fellow doesn't understand what pillows are for."

Mrs Morris looked suspiciously at Monkey Onassis. "I swear if that furry fiend could smile, he'd be grinning from hairy ear to hairy ear right now with what I let him get away with. Sometimes I think he does it just to get my goat."

"You haven't got a goat, Ma," said Maisie. Which was true.

"That's as maybe," said Mrs Morris. "But if I had one, he would get it, sure as eggs is eggs. Now, I shall have to get the Hoover out all over again."

"I'll do it, Ma," said Maisie putting down her book.

Mrs Morris smiled. "Oh, Maisie, you are a love. But I am not letting that monkey near anything electrical again, and besides, tomorrow is your first day back at school and you have a bag to pack and whatnot, I am sure. And *you* can shoo as well, Mr McDoon. I don't want you and your great gangly legs getting under my feet while I'm cleaning."

"Right you are, Mrs Morris," said Ramsey. "Come

on, Maisie, we can go to the rumpus room and watch some telly. There's jewellery on the shopping channel and I know the wee hairy creature likes the diamonds."

It was true. Monkey Onassis did love to look at anything sparkly, even if it was only on telly.

"OK," said Maisie, grabbing hold of him before Mrs Morris could change her mind and put him in his biscuit tin.

As they hopped down the stairs, she could just make out the sound of the Hoover exploding again.

"Hoop!" said Monkey Onassis proudly and smiled a monkey smile.

Back to School

The next morning Maisie sat at the breakfast table in her brand-new second-hand regulation St Regina's kilt, eating a bowl of Krispy Korny Flakes. Next to her sat Monkey Onassis, eating toast and jam very messily and without any use of knife or plate or table manners. And next to him sat Mrs Morris and all the residents of Withering Heights.

"Please, Ma," said Maisie, between mouthfuls of cereal. "Please let me take Monkey Onassis to school. He'll be on his best behaviour all day – I promise."

Mrs Morris looked at Monkey Onassis, who had blackberry and quince jam all over his fingers and was making purple patterns out of it on the white tablecloth.

"Not in a month of Sundays, my precious poppet," she said. "You are not taking that mess

24

magnet into a classroom. There'll be all manner of shenanigans, you'll be put into pretention and then, like as not, I'll get called to the school for raising a demonic daughter and keeping tropical creatures without a licence."

"It's *detention*, Ma," corrected Maisie. "And anyway, I've been teaching him all sorts. He can sit still for a whole fifteen minutes now and hold a pencil in his feet."

"I don't care if he can say his twelve times table while standing on his head; he is not going to school today," said Mrs Morris. "Besides, there'll be laws against it, I dare say. He might be carrying nits or Dutch elm disease. Maybe tomorrow, Maisie."

"But tomorrow never comes," protested Maisie.

"It did yesterday," pointed out Mrs Morris.

Maisie sighed and poked her cereal about a bit. There was no point arguing with her ma when she was in one of her moods. Monkey Onassis would have to stay behind all day.

"Don't worry, Maisie," said Loveday Pink, smiling a bright lipsticky smile at Maisie. "He can spend the

day with me. I'll find him something useful to do."
She turned to Monkey Onassis. "Won't I, young
fellow?"

Monkey Onassis looked at Loveday Pink, who
was wearing a tall hat made entirely of silvery blue
sequins that looked like a freshly caught pilchard. He
would have preferred to have spent the day with
Maisie, dismantling a hairdryer or stealing all the
plugs from the bathroom sinks, but as the alternative
would probably be being shut in his biscuit tin, he
decided he'd better co-operate.

"Hoop!" he said, spraying jammy toast crumbs all
over the table.

"Oh, I used to love school," said
Colonel Snell, stroking his waxed
military moustache fondly. "We used
to get six of the best with a wet
slipper just for looking as if we might
be unruly. Splendid stuff! Is it like that at
St Regina's?"

"Er, not really," said Maisie. "My old teacher, Miss
Stringfellow, says that teachers aren't allowed to be
violent any more – or they get sued or sacked –
and that making pictures out of macaroni is much

more therapeutic." Although Maisie secretly thought that some of her more rotten classmates could do with a good thwack with a wet slipper.

"Oh dear," said Colonel Snell. "Well, never mind, eh? Maybe your new teacher will be more fun – now you're moving up a class."

"Oh yes," said Loveday Pink. "What's she like?"

Maisie put down her spoon and thought for a second. "I'm not sure," she said. "Her name is Miss Bruton and she's new to the school, so no one knows her at all. But Miss Stringfellow said that at her last school her class won the Best-Dressed, Quietest and Most Likely to Be Doctors and Lawyers Under-Nines County Cup, so I am sure she is very good."

"Well, dearie," said Mrs Morris, collecting up the breakfast plates with a clatter. "Just be your usual self and I am sure she will like you."

Maisie nodded. She certainly hoped so. Because otherwise, St Regina's would be an awfully trouble-some place to be.

St Regina's

St Regina's was small and a bit fusty. It did not have rows of gleaming computers or an Olympic-sized swimming pool or the sort of teachers who let you call them "Dave" or "Shandy", or any of the other modern and new-fangled things which I am sure your primary school is full of.

It had seven classrooms – one for each year of children. It had a playground with hopscotch and a faded netball court. It had a caretaker, Mr Grimes, who waited at the gates to spot any dawdlers or shilly-shalliers. And it had a headmaster, Mr Peason, who found children a bit of an annoyance and spent most of the day dreaming of adventures in his caravan, a brand-new "Cleethorpes Comet".

Mostly, Maisie liked school. She liked reading, because in books all sorts of things were possible, such as talking animals and wizards. She liked

geography, because she learned all about other exciting places outside Groutley, like Northampton and Birmingham and Leamington Spa. She even liked the school dinners, except on a Thursday when it was sago for pudding, which looked like frogspawn and tasted a bit like it as well.

But there were three things that she did not like, not one bit. They were Belinda Braithwaite and her friends Lindy and Mindy Trotter.

Belinda was the daughter of Preston Braithwaite, the Groutley biscuit baron. 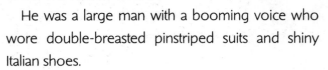 He owned a large factory on Timbuktu Road which made packets of custard creams, chocolate digestives and those horrid pink wafer things that always get left till last in an assortment box.

He was a large man with a booming voice who wore double-breasted pinstriped suits and shiny Italian shoes.

"Belinda, my treasure," he would say, "there is

only one thing more important in life than having money. And that is making sure everyone *knows* that you have it."

He spoiled Belinda rotten. For Christmas he had bought her a pogo stick, four pairs of pointy shoes and a parakeet called Britney. As a result Belinda was a revoltingly mean little madam. Her favourite pastime was being awful to Maisie on the grounds that she did not own a pogo stick or a parakeet, her Ma did not have a wardrobe full of fancy fur coats and, as for her father ... well, Maisie didn't have one of those at all.

The Trotter twins, Lindy and Mindy, were not as spoiled or as rich as Belinda but were no less obnoxious. They wore whatever Belinda wore, followed Belinda everywhere, bullied whoever Belinda bullied and agreed with every single word Belinda said.

When Maisie arrived at St Regina's for her first day back at school, they were already in the classroom, comparing their suntans.

Belinda had spent a whole month somewhere with palm trees and coconuts and drinks with pink umbrellas in them. Lindy and Mindy had had a week in Bournemouth, which was not as exotic but still a lot more interesting than Groutley.

"I'm as brown as a Chocobar!" Belinda was boasting excitedly. "Because I had a special servant just to rub lotion on my legs."

"We had one too," Lindy and Mindy lied. "But there are two of us so we only got half as brown each."

But before they could show off any more, Maisie came through the door.

"Oh, look, it's Manky Maisie!" screeched Belinda, her eyes lighting up like cheap fairy lights. "Where did you go this summer, Maisie?"

"Down to the bottom of Groutley High Street and back, I expect," said Lindy, hands on her hips.

"That's why she's as pasty as a pint of milk," added Mindy.

"Sunbathing's bad for you," said Maisie quietly.

"Don't be stupid," snapped Belinda. "You're just too poor to sunbathe. You were probably busy cleaning toilets like your stinky ma."

"Manky Maisie! Manky Maisie!" they all chorused.

Maisie glared at them. "I had more fun this summer than any of you have had in your whole lifetimes," she said.

"Oh, really?" said Belinda, rolling her eyes at Lindy and Mindy. "I don't see how. Old people just smell of cat wee and cabbage and talk about the war all day."

"And they have stupid haircuts," said Lindy meanly.

"And they wear overcoats – even in summer," added Mindy.

Now, as I am sure you know, Maisie was a quiet, kind girl who was not given to arguing or shouting

34

at people, but she did not like it when anyone said spiteful things about the old people at Withering Heights. Her face began to go red and she could feel a sort of twitching feeling in her feet and fingers until finally...

"Shut up the lot of you!" she cried.

Belinda, Lindy and Mindy, who had never seen Maisie raise so much as an eyebrow, let alone her voice, were so shocked that they did just that.

"You wouldn't know real fun if it came up and bit you on the backside," continued Maisie, still raging. "If you really want to know what I did this summer, then I shall tell you. I met the most marvellous magician called—"

But she stopped suddenly. Something was wrong. The entire class was silent and still. In fact, no one was even looking at Maisie any more. Instead they were staring over her right shoulder at the door with their mouths gaping open. And the room seemed to have got darker somehow.

"What is it?" asked Maisie. "Why are you all sitting down and why is no one answering back?"

"Because you should all have your scrawny bottoms on your seats and your mouths glued shut when I arrive, you insolent little squirt!" barked an alarming voice behind her.

Maisie swung round in shock. Standing in the doorway, blocking out all the daylight, was the most menacing woman Maisie had ever seen. She was almost as wide as she was tall, her eyes were black as ink and in her hand was a black leather Gladstone bag with the initials N.B. stamped on it in faded gold lettering.

Norma Bruton had arrived.

MS Bruton

Bullies come in all shapes and sizes.

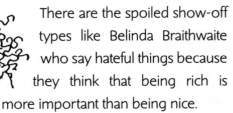

There are the spoiled show-off types like Belinda Braithwaite who say hateful things because they think that being rich is more important than being nice.

Then there are the big, thuggish sort who stamp on and squish smaller children because they are too stupid to know that it is wrong. I am sure you've met one or two of them.

But the good news about bullies is that most of them grow out of it by the time they leave school.

"Well, thank goodness for that!" I hear you say. "Because I am quite tired of Michelle Muttonchop poking fun at me."

But wait. I said *most*. Unfortunately, there are one

37

or two of these awful people who carry on stepping on smaller and quieter people all of their lives. Norma Bruton was one such person.

Norma had never been a beauty. When she was little, her teeth stuck out in odd directions and her feet were far too big for her age.

To make matters worse, she had four enormously gorgeous older brothers – Ned, Ted, Ed and Fred – who were all tall, blonde, sporting types.

The Bruton boys liked nothing better than helping little old ladies across the road before beating off all comers in a game of tennis. And when they weren't doing good deeds or winning trophies, they modelled swimwear for a catalogue.

Everyone loved them. Everyone, that is, except Norma. She hated their blonde curls and their long, lithe legs. She hated their normal-sized feet and their goody-two-shoes habits. But most of all she hated the fact that whenever they were around, no one took any notice of her at all.

So she decided to find something she was good at – something to make her stand out from the crowd.

That something was bullying, and she excelled at it.

She especially liked bullying children, because they were too scared to answer back. And in particular, she liked to bully the sort of children that everyone else loved – sweet, blonde, kind children. Children who reminded her of her brothers, Ned, Ted, Ed and Fred. Children exactly like Maisie Morris.

Ms Bruton eyed Maisie with the sort of look that a lion gives to a wildebeest before gulping it down whole.

"What's your name?" she demanded, dropping her black leather bag on her desk with an almighty smack.

"Maisie," whispered Maisie.

"Maisie what?" snorted Ms Bruton, leaning over to peer down at her. "Marvellous Maisie? Maisie the Magnificent?"

Maisie shivered. "No, Miss. Just Maisie Morris."

"It's not *Miss*, it's *Ms*," barked Ms Bruton right into Maisie's left ear. "And you, Maisie Morris, had jolly well better remember it or you'll be in even more hot water than you are already. I can tell you are the lead troublemaker in this class, so I shall be keeping my beady eyes on you, shan't I?"

"No, Miss. Honestly, Miss. I'm ever so good," said Maisie.

Ms Bruton's beady eyes turned as black as lumps of coal in a scuttle.

"It's Ms, you no-brained nincompoop. And in any case small children should only speak when spoken to."

"But you did speak to me," said Maisie. Which was true.

"Right, that's it, you undisciplined ignoramus,"

snapped Ms Bruton, standing up straight again so that she towered over Maisie like a giantess. "You can sit on your own at the dunce's desk right next to me where I can see you every second of the day."

Maisie did as she was told.

"Now listen to me, you halfwitted half-pints," said Ms Bruton, turning to the rest of the class. "You can forget whatever Miss Stringfellow has told you. From now on we do things by my rules – all forty-seven of them. There will be no talking, no eating, no gazing idiotically out of the window and most definitely no getting up to go to the toilet – you'll just have to hold on to it. I don't like chatterboxes, know-it-alls, bossy boots or clever clogs and I especially do not like creeps or snitches. Do I make myself clear?"

The class went to say "yes" but then thought better of it and just nodded instead.

"Good," said Ms Bruton. "Because I do not want to have to open up my big black leather bag and show you my instruments of punishment. I shall merely assure you they are long and pointy and extremely painful."

Maisie gulped and looked at the ominous black

bag. Ms Bruton saw her and smiled to herself.

"Right, you little losers," she continued, "time for some work. You have half an hour to write a page on 'What I did this summer'. It shouldn't be too taxing, as I expect most of it will say 'watched television' or 'ate sweets' since you are clearly all too stupid to do anything of any interest or importance. Your time starts ... *now*." She clicked a stopwatch, which hung upside down on her vast bosom, and settled back in her chair, one eye fixed firmly on Maisie.

Maisie chewed the end of her pencil. Things had gone from bad to worse. Not only was she now thought of as the class menace but, if she wrote about what had really happened that summer, then Ms Bruton would never believe her and she would get punished or tortured or, worse, sent to St Strangeway's Home for Horrible Girls – a large and gloomy institution run by a band of pitiless, military nuns called the Sisters of No Mercy.

But Mrs Morris had always told her to be honest and not to tell lies, not even incy-wincy ones. And if she caught wind of any fibbing, then there would be all manner of telling-off. It was tricky indeed.

But of course, in the end, there was only one thing a girl like Maisie could do. She took a big breath and started to write.

Maisie's Tale

"Right, that's it, time's up," said Ms Bruton, clicking her stopwatch. "Anyone who doesn't put down their pencil this instant will find it inserted very painfully into their nostrils."

Thirty pencils clattered noisily onto desks.

"Now, who's first?" said Ms Bruton, looking menacingly around the class. "You," she said, pointing to a small boy with spectacles. "What's your name?"

"Armitage Hopkins, Miss – I mean Ms," said Armitage.

"Right then, Hopkins, stand on your chair and read out what you've written."

Oh no, thought Maisie. Not Armitage. Anyone but him.

Armitage was a short, shy boy who

got picked on a lot on account of his having a glass eye. He also had diabetes, which meant he couldn't eat sweets like other children. His nickname was "sugar-free cyclops" which is exceptionally mean, and I expect you can guess which class bully first called him that.

Armitage climbed carefully onto his chair and looked around nervously.

"Come on, boy. What's the matter? Look me in the eye when I'm talking to you," said Ms Bruton.

Now there are some good things about having a glass eye. For instance, you can take it out and drop it in someone else's dinner so that it stares back at them when they get to the bottom of the gravy. Or you can hold it out in your hand and see round tricky corners that no one else can. But mostly, having a glass eye is annoying because it doesn't always point in the right direction, and the more nervous you get, the worse the eye wanders.

Right now, Armitage Hopkins was more nervous than he had ever been in his life.

"Hopkins, you have precisely three seconds to start reading out your essay before you get marched straight to Mr Peason. And there'll be no moaning to your ma about your mean new teacher either. I warn you, I am as tough with pleading parents as I am with their lazy offspring. Right, I'm starting now, three ... two..."

But before she got to one, Armitage could take no more and promptly wet himself in horror.

"Yeeeeegh!" screeched Belinda.

Oh no, thought Maisie.

"Sorry, Ms," said Armitage and started crying.

Ms Bruton looked as if she might possibly explode. "Get to the bathroom at once you weak-bladdered, lily-livered, one-eyed pest," she screeched.

Armitage didn't need telling twice and ran wailing out of the classroom.

Ms Bruton swung round to look at the rest of the children. "If anyone else thinks they can get out of this by turning on the waterworks, then they have another think coming. Now who's next?" Her eyes fixed on Maisie. "Maisie Morris," she said, smiling. "You seemed to have a lot to say for yourself earlier, so you can put your over-enthusiastic mouth to good use right now."

Maisie gulped. This was the worst thing that could happen. Why, oh why, oh why, did she say those stupid things to Belinda?

"Come on, child," said Ms Bruton. "What are you waiting for? Christmas?"

Maisie shook her head and clambered onto her chair.

"'What I did this summer' by Maisie Morris," she mumbled.

"Speak up!" snapped Ms Bruton.

Maisie took a deep breath. "This summer I met a magician with a monkey in a biscuit tin. The monkey stole diamonds but the magician caught him and made him stop thieving. He helped me and my ma get rid of the owners of the old people's home where I live by shrinking them into babies. Now everyone has fun instead of just watching TV all day. When the magician went away, I got to keep the monkey and now he lives with me in a laundry basket. His favourite foods are toast and fish fingers, and he also likes to play cards, but sometimes he eats them as well. The end."

Maisie looked up. Belinda was covering her mouth, trying not to laugh. Lindy and Mindy were twitching in their seats, barely able to contain themselves, and several other children's mouths were gaping open like fat frogs catching flies.

But worst of all was Ms Bruton, whose face had turned an interesting shade of purple and whose eyes were now darker than the Black Hole of Calcutta.

"Morris," said Ms Bruton, seething. "Are you deliberately trying to make a fool out of me?"

"No, Ms Bruton," said Maisie.

"Well then, are you mad?"

Belinda snorted behind her hand.

"No, Ms Bruton," said Maisie.

"In that case I can only assume that you are a compulsive liar who should be punished accordingly."

"But, Ms Bruton," protested Maisie, "it's true. I really do have a monkey. He's called Monkey Onassis and I really did get him from a magician."

"She's lying!" screeched Belinda, unable to keep silent any longer. "She's too poor to own a monkey."

"Liar, liar, pants on fire!" chorused Lindy and Mindy, jumping up and down.

"Silence!" snapped Ms Bruton. "I can smell a

whopper at twenty paces and I don't need any help from you three twerps."

Belinda, Lindy and Mindy sat down sulkily, pulling faces at Maisie as they did.

"Right then, Morris," continued Ms Bruton. "You can have one last chance to confess, or I will have no choice but to punish you."

Maisie thought for a second. What if she were to pretend it was a lie? Would that be as bad as having lied in the first place? But then, it wasn't a lie. She did own a monkey and she had beaten the Awful Arkwrights. So why should she have to say it was a fib?

"It's the truth," she said quietly.

Ms Bruton grabbed Maisie by the scruff of her regulation cardigan and carried her off the chair and straight out of the door. She marched down the corridor to Mr Grimes's store cupboard, opened the door and dropped Maisie inside with a thump.

"Now you listen to me, you little villain!" she hissed, leaning over Maisie so that Maisie could smell her breath, which was like old socks. "I have reduced boys three times your size to weeping wimps for daring to cheek me in class and I do not

like being made a laughing-stock by someone as small and insignificant as you. Do you understand?"

Maisie nodded.

"Then I shall let you out at the end of the afternoon, when you have learned your lesson."

"But what about lunch?" said Maisie.

Ms Bruton smiled a nasty smile. "I am sure there are some nice crunchy cockroaches in there, or a tasty mouse or two." And with that she slammed the door, leaving Maisie on her own in the dark.

The cupboard was damp and cold and smelled of disinfectant and wet dog. As Maisie sat down on the edge of Mr Grimes's tin bucket, a tear began to worm its way out of her right eye and roll slowly down her cheek. This was not a good start to term at all. Belinda Braithwaite was as mean and spiteful as ever, her new teacher was an ogress and, worse, what was she going to say to her ma when she got home? And what, exactly, was Mrs Morris going to say to her?

Ramsey's Story

"Holy Moses, Maisie, you've only been back at school five minutes and you're causing pandemonium, hullabaloo and who knows what else! As if I haven't got enough to worry about, what with Mr Nidgett's glue ear and that dratted monkey of yours, who has not been on his best behaviour all day, not one jot," was what Mrs Morris had to say to her.

While Maisie had been at school, Monkey Onassis had pulled all the sequins off Loveday's pilchard hat creating a fantastic glimmery rain shower. Then he had fiddled with the controls on the Twitchett twins' hearing aids, which meant everyone had had to shout, giving Mrs Morris a headache. And

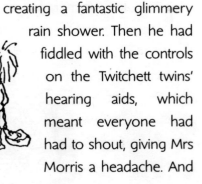

as if that was not enough, he had dropped one of his plastic toys into the tea urn and Mrs Morris had scorched her arm trying to get it out for him.

As punishment, Monkey Onassis had only been allowed dried crackers for lunch and had spent the rest of the afternoon shut in his biscuit tin.

"But all I did was tell the truth, Ma," said Maisie.

"I am sure you did, my duck, and you know how I can't abide lies, but couldn't you have just told her a bit less truth? Honestly, Maisie, you know I love you, but right now I've got twenty-three assorted pensioners to look after, plus a deranged monkey, so I need you to be on your double-best behaviour. And another thing," she added, "your shoes smell of pneumonia and you're all covered in cobwebs. How the giddy aunt did you manage that?"

"Ms Bruton locked me in the store cupboard as punishment," said Maisie.

Mrs Morris glared at her. "Maisie Morris, are you telling fibs? I'm sure teachers aren't allowed to do that sort of thing any more. Like as not, you got in there yourself with that awful Braithwaite girl. You stay away from her, Maisie. She'll lead you up the wrong garden path and no mistake. I ask you, why does a girl of that age need her hair tinted and her nails manicured and probably her eyelashes permed as well? I just don't know."

Maisie sighed and trod wearily upstairs to her bedroom to let Monkey Onassis out of the tin.

Monkey Onassis was delighted at Maisie's return. He hooked his arms around her neck and hooped into her ear softly to show how much he loved her.

"Let's go and see Ramsey," said Maisie. "He'll understand."

And with Monkey Onassis still round her neck she went back down the turret stairs and along the landing to Ramsey McDoon's room.

"Och, no one ever believed me at school either," said Ramsey. "They said I was lying when I told them my father was once the midget strongman of the Highlands. 'The Mighty Flea' was his name, God rest his soul. It was the same even when I was Chief of Police. Tell me, Maisie, have you ever heard of the Black Annis?"

Maisie shook her head.

"Aye well, she was an evil beastie that haunted the

54

Highlands. A fearsome hag with claws made of iron. She lived in a cave she had hollowed out herself with her claws, and stole human children to boil them up for soup."

Maisie shuddered. Even Ms Bruton wasn't *that* bad.

"Well, one day I saw her," said Ramsey. "Gigantic she was; her claws shining in the Scottish sun; her black cloak billowing out behind."

"Crikey!" said Maisie. "What did you do?"

"Well, I ran away, of course," said Ramsey. "Straight back to the police station to tell everyone. The whole town marched up to the glen with shotguns and clubs and pitchforks, but she was gone. And, of course, everyone thought I'd been making it up. No evidence of her, you see. I needed concrete proof – a bit of her cloak or something."

"Did you ever see her again?" asked Maisie.

"Och aye," said Ramsey. "But I never told anyone. No point – not without evidence. And ever since that day, no one has believed a word I say."

That night, as she lay in her bed in the turret, Maisie thought to herself about Ramsey's story. Of course no one believed her. Who would believe that a monkey lived in Groutley? After all, nothing exciting ever happened here. She needed evidence. That was what Ramsey had been missing all those years.

She looked down at Monkey Onassis, who was snug in his laundry basket, wearing one of Maisie's old vests, and smiled. While he might not be made of concrete, Maisie certainly had proof. Very real and furry proof. There was only one thing for it: she would have to take Monkey Onassis to school. After all, her ma hadn't exactly said that he could *never* go to school. She said he wasn't to go to school *today* and today was over now.

"You'd like to go to school, wouldn't you?" whispered Maisie.

Monkey Onassis thought about this and nodded.

That was settled then. Easy-peasy, thought Maisie to herself.

But nothing with Monkey Onassis was ever that easy, as Maisie was about to find out.

Monkey Onassis goes to School

"Please, Monkey Onassis, please get in the tin. It's already after eight and we have to leave for school."

Maisie was already dressed and was hopping from one foot to the other with impatience.

But Monkey Onassis did not want to co-operate and sat in the corner of the turret with his back to Maisie and his fur puffed out so that he looked like a gigantic pom-pom. He would much rather be carried to school on Maisie's shoulder where he could watch cars and bicycles whizz past on the way.

"Pleeease," begged Maisie again. "I'll give you my crisps." And she shook her bag of Prawn Ringos so that Monkey Onassis could hear.

Monkey Onassis turned his head slightly and looked at Maisie with one eye. He liked crisps. He liked the crunchy, crackly sound they made in his mouth, and he especially liked the big bang they

made when he jumped up and down on the packet to open it – another of his habits that Mrs Morris was not too fond of.

But he still wouldn't get in the tin.

"Oh, very well, I will let you play on my roller skates for two whole hours after school," said Maisie, holding them up so he could see.

Even more than crisps, Monkey Onassis liked whizzing up and down the carpets at Withering Heights on one of Maisie's roller skates.

He sidled up to them and touched one lovingly with his hand.

59

"Is that a deal?" asked Maisie.

Monkey Onassis thought it was and climbed inside his tin.

"Thank goodness," said Maisie and with the tin under one arm she ran down the stairs, nearly tripping over her ma, who was busy dusting the landing.

"Maisie Morris, where are you going at that speed? You'll have your eye out on the banisters if you're not careful!" shrieked Mrs Morris, waving a tin of polish and a duster at Maisie.

"School, Ma," said Maisie, hiding the tin behind her back hurriedly. "I mustn't be late, or Ms Bruton might lock me in the cupboard again."

"What have I told you about fibs?" said Mrs Morris. "Honestly, I don't know what's got into you this term, Maisie. And just you stay out of bother today. If I catch wind of any more mischief, then I may very well spontaneously compost."

"Yes, Ma. I promise, Ma," said Maisie. And she crossed her fingers for luck. She was going to need it.

Ms Bruton eyed the biscuit tin under Maisie's arm suspiciously as she walked into the classroom.

"What have you got there, Morris?" she said. "Don't think you can win me over with biscuits. I will not have them in the classroom. They rot your teeth, make too much noise and leave crumbs every-where. It's rule number 33."

Ms Bruton's rules – all forty-seven of them – were written in inky swirls next to the blackboard. As well as the NO BISCUITS rule, they included:

11. NO JEWELLERY (BOYS OR GIRLS)

19. NO FANCY HAIRDOS

21. NO CHEWING-GUM IN CLASS

22. NO CHEWING BIRO LIDS IN CLASS

29. NO PRETENDING THE DOG HAS EATEN YOUR HOMEWORK

41. NO DISAGREEING WITH MS BRUTON

42. NO EVEN THINKING THAT MS BRUTON COULD BE WRONG

Maisie was sure that NO MONKEYS IN TINS was probably in there somewhere but it was too late for that now. And besides, she had to prove that she wasn't a liar.

"It's not biscuits," she said.

"Well, whatever it is, I'm confiscating it," said Ms Bruton. "We are going on a class outing to the *Groutley Chronicle* and I don't want you fiddling with it while we're there."

Maisie gulped. This was not good. Not good at all.

Maisie usually liked class trips. Last year Miss Stringfellow had taken them to Groutley Wildlife Park to look at the animals – which consisted of a turtle, two otters and an ocelot with a limp.

The year before that they had been to Braithwaite's Biscuits to see how jammy dodgers were made. Bruce Luke had eaten so many of the free samples that he had been sick on the minibus on the way home and had to wear just his pants and vest for the rest of the day.

But today Maisie didn't feel like a visit at all.

"Are you deaf as well as stupid?" barked Ms Bruton. "I do hope not, because that would be breaking rule 46. Now give me that tin immediately, or I will forcibly remove it from you."

Her hands shaking, Maisie handed the tin to Ms Bruton, who opened the big jaws of her black leather bag, dropped it in and snapped the clasp shut.

"There," she said. "You can have it back after school."

Maisie looked at the bag. After school was a long time away, and Monkey Onassis was not used to being shut up for so long. It made him agitated. And when he got agitated, anything could happen.

"Right, you nasty little gnomes," said Ms Bruton to the class, "line up in twos and hold hands, and we'll march to the *Chronicle* in formation and utter silence."

Maisie looked around. Everyone had paired up already. There was no one left for her.

"Oh dear," said Ms Bruton. "All on your own again? Well, never mind, you can hold my hand." And she grabbed Maisie sharply.

"Ow!" said Maisie.

"What was that?" snapped Ms Bruton, glaring down at her.

"Nothing, Ms," said Maisie.

"Good," said Ms Bruton. "Now, left, right, quick march!"

And off they went, Maisie firmly gripped in Ms Bruton's gigantic claw and Monkey Onassis firmly shut in the teacher's black leather bag.

The Groutley Chronicle

"Listen up, small fry," said Ms Bruton. "No fiddling, no stealing and no asking idiotic questions. Keep quiet and listen to what the man in charge tells you. I shall be testing you on it later."

Maisie had never been inside a newspaper office before. It was a bustling room, full of computers and piles of paper. Four televisions were all tuned to different channels. Several men and women in cheap suits sat typing frantically with one hand and talking furiously into telephones at the same time. And in the middle of it all stood a large and greasy-looking man.

"Hello, everyone," he said. "My name is Lester Sylvester, editor in chief, top international correspondent and the man behind all the scoops here at the *Chronicle.*"

Lester liked school visits. Children were especially

easy to lie to. And it made him feel doubly important.

"This is the newsroom where my reporters make up – I mean *type up* – all the stories for tomorrow's paper," he continued. "Except the front page. Only I get to do that because only I am clever enough to know what is the top story of the day. And anything the reporters write gets checked by me personally as well."

"To make sure the facts are straight," said Ms Bruton to the class.

"Er, no," said Lester. "To make sure it's got enough good words in it. Facts don't sell newspapers, my dear, but imagination works wonders. Any questions?"

Thirty hands shot up in the air.

"No stupid ones!" barked Ms Bruton.

"Have you ever been to a war?" asked Belinda.

"Yes," lied Lester. "It was hot and loud and danger-ous and I got my arm blown clean off. It had to be stitched on again up a tree by a witch doctor while we sheltered from the enemy."

"Have you met anyone famous?" asked Lindy and Mindy.

"Yes," lied Lester again. "I have met the Queen. She invited me to the Palace especially, after I revealed that her lady-in-waiting was in fact a Russian spy called Irma Smirnoff."

Maisie put her hand up.

"Yes?" asked Lester.

"Isn't Groutley a bit dull after all that?" asked Maisie. "I mean, there are no wars or spies here."

Lester smiled at her, showing his nasty yellowing teeth. "What's your name, little girl?" he asked.

"Maisie Morris," said Maisie.

"Well, Maisie, you'd be surprised what I can dig up when I want to." And he winked at her. Maisie shuddered. There was something odd about Lester Sylvester. He looked like the sort of man who would try to sell his own grandma. Which in fact he had.

"Now follow me, children," said Lester, striding off across the office. "I will show you the printing press. But leave your coats and bags in my office. It's a large and potentially fatal machine and I don't want any buttons getting caught in the cogs, or you could end up as front-page news yourselves."

Maisie hung her anorak on a peg on the wall and watched as Ms Bruton dropped her black leather bag on the floor with a thud.

"Please be good, Monkey Onassis," said Maisie quietly.

"What are you muttering about, you nitwit?" snapped Ms Bruton.

"Nothing, Ms Bruton," said Maisie.

"Well, keep your trap shut from now on, or I shall stitch it shut for you with extra-strong catgut."

Maisie nodded gloomily. She had an awful feeling in the pit of her tummy. The sort you get when you have been stuck on the waltzer at the fairground after an extra-large helping of candyfloss.

Something was going to happen, she just knew it.
And she was right.

Monkey Onassis on the Loose

Monkey Onassis was fast asleep, dreaming of diamonds. He was just getting to a good bit involving the Crown Jewels and a strangely co-operative Beefeater at the Tower of London when his hairy bottom hit the floor with an enormous thud and he woke up.

It was dark. Darker than it had been when he went to sleep. And quiet. He couldn't hear Maisie at all. He peered through one of the holes in his biscuit tin but all he could see was blackness.

"Hoop!" he said very loudly. But no one replied.

Monkey Onassis did not like being shut up. He wanted to see Maisie.

"HOOP!" he shouted.

But there was still no answer. So he started to jump up and down in a very annoyed manner, shrieking as he did so until, eventually, the lid of his tin pinged off and the black leather bag burst open, sending its contents flying around Lester's office.

Out flew a bar of soap (to wash out the mouths of swearers). Out flew a set of handcuffs (for fidgety Phils). Out flew a reinforced ruler (to rap the knuckles of rotten-doers). And out flew Monkey Onassis, who landed on his bottom on top of a filing cabinet.

"Hoop," he said to himself grumpily and looked around. But he still couldn't see Maisie.

He opened up the top drawer of Lester's filing cabinet. In it he found Lester's lunch – two fish-paste sandwiches. But no Maisie. He ate one of the sandwiches and filed the other under E for ENVIRONMENTAL CATASTROPHES.

In Lester's desk he found a packet of gum, three pounds fifty and a signed photo of Lester's favourite singer, Johnny Sparkles, but still no Maisie. So he chewed some of the gum, which was horrid and stringy and got stuck in his teeth, took the money in case he needed it later and drew a big swirly moustache on the photograph in blue indelible pen.

Then he saw the computer. Monkey Onassis liked computers chiefly because he was not, under any circumstances, allowed to play on them, after an incident with some orange juice and a lot of smoke and sparks. He hopped onto the desk and sat down in front of the keyboard.

First of all he tapped several random letters in the middle of a story about a swarm of killer bees that had been spotted in a tree outside Fishcoteque takeaway. Then he pressed a red key marked FILE STORY, which made the words disappear from the screen. Then he banged his fists on lots of keys at once to see what happened but it made the computer screen freeze, so Monkey Onassis got bored, clambered down from the desk and scampered out of Lester's office in search of Maisie.

In the tea room he found four plastic coffee mugs with pictures of Lester on them and a microwave oven but no Maisie. So he put the mugs in the microwave and melted them, creating a lot of blue smoke and a smell like burnt hair.

In the toilets he found a bottle of Whizz Clean Citrus Foam Wash, which he poured down the toilet, making an alarming mess which foamed out of the toilet, across the floor and into the cloakroom, covering everyone's jackets in lemony bubbles.

In the stationery cupboard he found a gross of paper clips and twenty-four bottles of Indian ink but no Maisie. So he poured the paper clips out of their box and poured the ink in.

Then he heard something in the distance. A sort of whirring, clanking noise. It sounded interesting and just the sort of noise that Maisie liked as well. So he hopped out of the stationery cupboard and padded along the corridor to find it.

Stop Press

The printing press was a gigantic monster of a machine. It was black and shiny and taller than three elephants stacked on top of each other. It had several funnels to pour in the ink, a big stamper to print all the words on the pages and a conveyor belt to whizz the newspapers through.

Maisie looked at it in awe as it chugged and cranked.

"Impressive, isn't it?" said Lester. "It's the very latest model, fashioned entirely by midgets in the Welsh mountains from precious black iron ore." Which was a load of rubbish but Lester thought it sounded good.

Maisie nodded. "How does it know what to print?" she asked.

"Ah. Well, that's the real genius," said Lester. "Once I have made sure the stories are exciting enough,

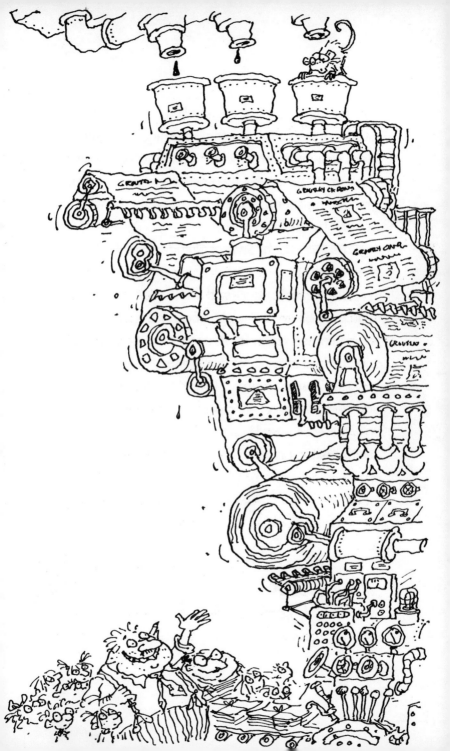

the computer checks the spelling, arranges them nicely so they all fit on the page and then sends them straight down to the machine to be printed. Look, you can see the latest news right here." Lester grabbed a paper as it hurtled past on the conveyor belt and handed it to Maisie.

"Coo! *Killer Beans Swarm Outside Top Takeaway,*" she read aloud.

"Killer beans? Hah!" said Ms Bruton to Maisie. "You must be blind as well as deaf and stupid, which is breaking several rules at once. Give it here!" And she grabbed the paper from Maisie.

"*Killer Beans Swarm...* Hmm. It does say that," admitted Ms Bruton, annoyed.

"What?" blustered Lester. "I didn't write that. Let me see." And he grabbed the paper from Ms Bruton.

It was the story that Monkey Onassis had fiddled with. He had added odd letters so that *killer bees* said *killer beets*. But the computer thought that beets were unseasonal so had changed it to *beans*.

"But beans aren't dangerous. They're not even scary," said Belinda knowingly.

"I know that!" snapped Lester. "*Bees*. It was meant to say *bees*. Someone has been tampering with my typing."

Maisie's heart skipped a beat. It couldn't be, could it?

But it was. And things were about to get worse.

Monkey Onassis had found his way to the printing press through a small air vent near the ink funnels. From his perch he had a magnificent view of the machine and, more importantly, Maisie.

"Hoop!" he squawked, trying to get her attention. But the printing press was too loud and Maisie couldn't hear him.

He decided he had to get down to her. So he hooked one end of his tail onto the edge of a funnel and let go of the air vent. Unfortunately, at that very moment, the machine decided it was running short on ink and opened a shutter above. *Whooosh!*

Monkey Onassis was washed down the funnel with the ink and disappeared inside.

The machine, not used to being full of monkey, gave an almighty groan.

"What was that?" said Lester, swinging round.

"Oh, please no," said Maisie to herself as it started to screech and rattle.

"Stand back, children!" ordered Ms Bruton.

"What the Dickens?" shouted Lester.

"My dad will sue you if anything happens to me!" said Belinda.

Lester was just about to say something very rude indeed when the machine gave an almighty cough and spat out a very black, wet and inky Monkey Onassis onto the conveyor belt.

"Hoop!" he shrieked at Maisie and began running the wrong way along the conveyor belt to reach her.

"It's a devil!" shouted Ms Bruton.

"It's a Welsh midget!" shouted Lester.

"No," said Maisie quietly, "it's Monkey Onassis."

"Hoop," said Monkey Onassis happily as he leaped off the conveyor belt and flung his arms round Maisie's neck.

Ms Bruton's eyes went blacker than the inky monkey.

"What did you say, Morris?" she thundered.

Maisie looked at her sorrowfully.

"It's my monkey," she said. "The one I told you about yesterday but no one believed me."

"Liar!" squawked Belinda. "She must have stolen it from the Wildlife Park last night. And that's rule number 41 she's just broken – NO DISAGREEING WITH YOU, Ms Bruton!"

"Shut up, Braithwaite," snapped Ms Bruton. "That's rule number 40 you've just broken – NO SPEAKING UNLESS SPOKEN TO." Then she turned back to Maisie. "What is that creature doing here?" she demanded.

"It's my evidence," said Maisie.

"Evidence of what?" snapped Ms Bruton. "That you

are horribly small and feeble-minded? Or that you are stupider than a llama with a lobotomy?"

"No," said Maisie, "that I'm not a liar."

"Hah!" shouted Ms Bruton. "All this proves is that you will go to any lengths to cover up one of your whoppers. You, Morris, are the worst child I have ever had the displeasure to come across and, believe me, I've met some very bad eggs in my time. You're a liar, a cheat and, what's worse, you have stolen a dangerous wild animal just to show off."

"I'm sorry," said Maisie.

"Sorry isn't good enough," said Ms Bruton, seething. "I'm calling your mother this instant. And you can thank your lucky stars my thwacking instruments are in Mr Sylvester's office or I'd give you a jolly good walloping right here."

"Yes, Ms Bruton," said Maisie.

"What about my machinery?" snapped Lester. "This could cost me millions."

"Don't exaggerate," thundered Ms Bruton. But then she looked at Maisie and had a thought. "I tell you what. I shall leave Morris here to clean up any mess she has made. And if she doesn't finish it today, she can come back after school tomorrow, and the day after that, and the day after that, until it's all sorted out."

"Hmm. Very well," said Lester. But he was not happy, not in the slightest.

Maisie's Punishment

Maisie sat in Lester's office with the filthy and bedraggled Monkey Onassis on her lap. Things had gone from bad to worse. Not only did everyone at St Regina's think she was a liar but now she had broken at least five of Ms Bruton's rules, Monkey Onassis had completely ransacked the *Groutley Chronicle* and her ma was about to arrive.

As if to confirm the enormity of the situation, Mrs Morris came bustling in at that very moment still wearing her rubber gloves and overall.

"Lawks-a-mussy, Maisie!" she cried. "What in the name of Jupiter have you done now?"

"I didn't mean to, Ma," said Maisie, and tears started to roll down her cheeks.

"Oh, my stars, don't cry," wailed Mrs Morris, clapping her yellow rubbery hands to her face. "I know you're in trouble but tears aren't going to help, are they?

Why on earth did you take that creature to school? I told you not to. He's trickier than a bagful of restless ferrets."

"Because no one believed me," said Maisie. "And they still don't. Now they think I *stole* him."

"You're lucky I didn't call the police," said Lester.

"The police?" gasped Mrs Morris. "Oh, Maisie, you're going to be locked up with all those awful gangsters and criminals and like as not you'll end up with tattoos and a degree in lock-breaking!"

"Not for her," said Lester. "For the monkey. Anyway, I didn't."

"A good job as well," said Mrs Morris. "He's probably wanted dead or alive for all those wretched diamonds he stole."

"Diamonds?" said Lester, suddenly very interested.

"Ooh yes," said Mrs Morris. "He's a terror for the gems."

"Really?" said Lester, rubbing his sweaty palms together. "Really?" Then he shook himself, as if he had been dreaming. "Anyway. You had better get that horrible, hairy Houdini out of here so Maisie can start cleaning."

"I certainly shall," said Mrs Morris. "Come here,

you fiendish imp. Get in your tin. It's in the bath and then straight to bed for you – with no fish fingers."

Monkey Onassis looked up at Maisie with a sorry look on his black face.

"Go on," said Maisie. "You have to go."

"Hoop," said Monkey Onassis sadly and he climbed reluctantly back in his tin.

"Right, I shall be off," said Mrs Morris, slamming the lid down firmly. "And don't expect any supper when *you* get home either, Maisie. You are not in my good books at all." And she stomped out of the office, leaving Maisie on her own with Lester.

"So, a jewel thief, eh?" said Lester, reclining in his big leather swivel chair and plopping his feet on the desk.

"Yes," said Maisie, who was kneeling on the floor, picking up the contents of Lester's in-tray, which had been scattered about the office during Monkey Onassis's escape.

"Well, maybe I'll write a story about him one day," said Lester.

"I think he'd like that," said Maisie. "He's always wanted to be famous."

"Really?" said Lester. "Well, I'm the man who can –

as they say." Then he lit one of his cigarettes. "Right, twinkle toes, I am off to shout at some reporters, so finish cleaning and then you can run along home."

"OK," said Maisie.

Then Lester bent down so that his cigarette dangled dangerously in Maisie's face.

"And don't touch the computer," he said. "It's extremely complicated and not for small girls."

"Yes, sir," said Maisie. Then Lester smiled, puffed a ring of smoke into Maisie's face and walked out.

Maisie did as she was told. She cleaned and polished and swept and scrubbed until the office was cleaner than it had ever been. Only one thing was still messy: the computer screen had a large blob of something that looked suspiciously like monkey spit stuck on it.

Maisie looked around. Lester was busy outside giving a young sports correspondent a very loud talking-to.

I'd better wipe it off, thought Maisie to herself and she leaned over the enormous desk to reach the screen.

But when she had wiped it clean, she saw something underneath that was even more horrible.

86

"Oh, heavens, no," she said to herself.

But heavens, yes! Because there on the screen was a large and, frankly, unbelievable headline.

"MACAROON MADNESS! GROUTLEY BISCUIT BARON DOES A BUNK!" it thundered in gigantic capitals. And underneath, in smaller print, "*Preston Braithwaite disappeared in decidedly dodgy circumstances yesterday after the shocking revelation that he has been poisoning his famous biscuits. The alarm was raised by an anonymous* Chronicle *reader, who told us, 'It was terrible. First my tongue*

87

turned blue, then I got the galloping trots.' She put it down to a Braithwaite's garibaldi at elevenses. Other fans of the snacks are being warned to chuck out their cheese crackers and ditch their digestives for fear that rogue packets may still be at large."

At first Maisie thought Monkey Onassis had fiddled with another story. Now, there is an ancient and wise saying: "If you sit enough monkeys down at enough computers, then one of them will write a Shakespearean sonnet"; but I can assure you that Monkey Onassis was *not* that monkey. And Maisie knew it.

"Then it must be true!" she said to herself. "Crikey! Just wait till I tell Ma!" And she ran to grab her anorak and bag off the hooks.

"Are you still here?" thundered Lester, appearing at the doorway.

"Er, yes. I mean no," said Maisie, zipping herself up. "I'm going now."

"Well, shoo then!" said Lester. "I've got important work to do. And he sat himself down at the computer and swung round on his chair.

Bursting with her news, Maisie walked quickly up

Groutley High Street. Past Totally Trousers, past Fishcoteque takeaway, past Flash Legs Kung Fu video shop and up towards the Brentville bypass.

She was just about to turn right along William Hague Way when a large, white limousine pulled up next to her and two tinted windows rolled down.

Oh no, thought Maisie. But oh yes. It was Belinda Braithwaite, wearing bright blue eyeshadow and sucking a toffee apple.

"Enjoy your cleaning, did you?" she hooted. "Now you're just like your ma! Manky Maisie!"

Poor Belinda, thought Maisie. She can't have heard yet.

"And don't think you can keep that monkey either," added Belinda. "My dad says he's going to buy it for me."

"That I will, my precious," said a booming voice from the driver's seat.

Maisie looked in. Then she looked harder just to make sure. Her face turned pale. Because sitting there, larger than life, was the biscuit baron himself, Preston Braithwaite, his suit striped like a deckchair and gold rings spangling on every finger.

"And I'll thank you to stay away from my daughter," he said to Maisie. "I've heard you're a troublemaker and I won't have my baby Belinda corrupted by the likes of you, you commoner!"

"B–b–but you've not disappeared at all!" said Maisie.

"Disappeared?" thundered Preston. "Why would someone as successful and good-looking as I am disappear? You are clearly as idiotic as my beautiful Belinda says you are."

And with that, he rolled up the windows and zoomed off down the road, leaving Maisie in a cloud of exhaust and confusion.

"I don't understand," Maisie said to Monkey Onassis as they sat on the bed in the turret that night, their tummies rumbling after their no suppers. "It was there in black and white on Lester's computer screen. I'm sure of it."

But then Maisie thought hard again. "No," she said to Monkey Onassis, "I must have misread it. After all, Lester wouldn't make stories up. Would he?"

Monkey Onassis shrugged his shoulders and scratched his damp fur glumly. He was feeling very sore and sorry for himself since Mrs Morris had scrubbed him with scouring powder to get rid of the ink – and he smelled distinctly of scullery.

"Goodnight, Monkey Onassis," said Maisie. "Tomorrow will be a better day, I promise."

But as she lay in the dark in the spindly turret, Maisie couldn't help feeling that it wasn't over yet. There was something about Lester Sylvester that made her go all cold and clammy, as if she had dipped her hands in blancmange.

He was up to something. Just what she didn't know yet. But she was going to find out, sure as eggs is eggs.

Biscuit Mania

"Glory be!" shrieked Mrs Morris, charging into the breakfast room, her hair sticking out every which way. "It's Biscuit Armageddon. We've all been poisoned by jammy dodgers and dodgy wafers."

"What, Ma?" asked Maisie, who was drinking her milk and trying to stop Monkey Onassis pouring his into the peanut butter pot.

"Barbara from bingo has been on the phone," Mrs Morris continued. "Apparently it's all over the paper. Preston Braithwaite has put poison in his biscuits. He's in hiding and we're all going to turn blue and who knows what else!"

She threw her hands in the air.

"I'll have to empty the cupboards, and you must check upstairs as well – I know that monkey stole some caramel snaps yesterday. Lord above knows he's in my bad books but I don't want to see

him dead – or worse."

Maisie wondered what could be worse than dead. But then she remembered what she had seen.

"But that can't be right," she said.

"What?" said Mrs Morris as she threw a packet of rich tea fingers into the dustbin.

"It wasn't a real story," said Maisie. "It was a mistake. And in any case, I saw him."

"Saw who? What are you wittering on about when there're deadly biscuits to be dispatched."

"Mr Braithwaite," said Maisie. "I saw him last night on my way home. He hadn't disappeared at all."

"Of course not," said Mrs Morris. "That must have been before word got out about the poison. I knew something suspicious was going on – those Twitchett twins have had the trots for two days and you know how they like their garibaldis."

Maisie thought for a minute. It still didn't make sense. She needed to see a copy of the paper, and fast.

"Do we have today's *Chronicle*, Ma?" she asked.

"Cripes no, love. It's all gossip and tittle-tattle, and I get that from Barbara so I don't need to pay for it," said Mrs Morris and stamped on a particularly menacing-looking bourbon.

94

Maisie made a mental list of everyone in Withering Heights who might get the paper delivered. She ruled out Loveday Pink, as she only read romance novels with titles like *Doctor of Destiny* or *Lost in Love* and pictures of couples clutching each other on windswept beaches or hospital car parks on the cover. Bristow Muldoon was too short-sighted to tell the difference between a newspaper and toilet paper, so it wouldn't be him.

Colonel Snell took *Green-Fingered and Gung Ho: The Journal of the Royal Emergency Gardening Battalion* but not the *Groutley Chronicle*.

Then she remembered. Ramsey McDoon! He read it religiously to check how his football team, Tongue-Twisters FC, were doing. He would have a copy.

Maisie grabbed Monkey Onassis and ran up the stairs and along the landing to his bedroom, where she knocked on the door.

"Who's there?" asked Ramsey.

"It's me – Maisie," said Maisie. "Can I come in?"

"Aye, of course," said Ramsey.

Maisie pushed open the door. Ramsey was sitting up in bed in a string vest, drinking beef tea – and reading the paper!

"What can I do for you, lassie?" asked Ramsey.

"I need to check something in the *Chronicle*, if I can, please," replied Maisie.

"Och – worried your little caper with Monkey Onassis made it to the front page, I expect," said Ramsey, laughing. "Well, don't you go bothering yourself, little lady, not a word of it in here. Just the usual council matters. Oh, and something about some poisoned biscuits."

Maisie gulped. "Say that again!" she said.

"Aye, did ye not hear aboot it? Preston Braithwaite's vanished. Awful business. Reminds me of the time when I nearly caught the famous—"

But Maisie wasn't listening. "Show me the front page!" she said.

"OK, OK," said Ramsey and held it up for her to see.

There it was in black and white. The exact same story she had read last night on Lester Sylvester's computer. Word for word.

"But he couldn't have known," said Maisie.

"What's that, lassie?" asked Ramsey.

"The story. I read it yesterday afternoon on Lester Sylvester's computer."

"Well, of course you did, lassie. He wrote it," said Ramsey.

"No, you don't understand," said Maisie. "First I read it at the *Chronicle*. Then I saw Preston Braithwaite later that afternoon. He hadn't disappeared at all; he was in his big car, driving up Groutley High Street with Belinda. So how could Lester have known about something that hadn't even happened yet?"

"Maybe he has special powers and can see into the future," said Ramsey. "Like one of those Gypsy women, only without the crystal ball – or the earrings."

"No," said Maisie. If there was one thing she knew about Lester it was that there was nothing magical about him whatsoever.

"Maybe he got a tip-off – a phone call from the biscuit inspectors, eager for publicity," said Ramsey.

"No," said Maisie. "He was with us all afternoon and he didn't answer the phone once."

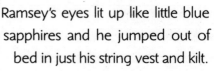

Ramsey's eyes lit up like little blue sapphires and he jumped out of bed in just his string vest and kilt.

"By golly, girlie!" he said, hopping around the bedroom carpet. "Groutley's very own mystery! It may only be biscuits but by gumbo we'll solve it! Now first of all we need more clues."

"How do we get those?" said Maisie, her own eyes wide as saucers.

Ramsey stroked his ginger beard and thought hard.

"Well, we must start at the beginning," he said. "That means we need to take a look at Lester's compooter!"

"But Lester will never let me back into the *Chronicle* after the mess Monkey Onassis made." And she glared hard at him.

"Don't be hard on the wee hairy chappie," said Ramsey. "If it wasn't for that mess, you would never have seen the biscuit story!"

It was true. Maisie squeezed Monkey Onassis's paw to say sorry.

"Hoop!" he replied, proud to be part of the mystery.

"Anyway, we've no need to go back," said Ramsey. "We can do the work from here."

"But how?" said Maisie, confused.

Ramsey smiled. "With my compooter of course." And he pointed to one sat on his dressing table next to his vase of thistles.

"Hoop!" squawked Monkey Onassis in excitement, eyeing the big white machine with delight.

"It's a wondrous invention, the compooter," said

Ramsey. "I can have super chats with people all over the world. Why, only last night I discussed how to catch French fugitives with a beautiful Parisian policewoman called Belladonna. Quite charming she was! Of course, she thinks I'm thirty-five, incredibly rich and a spy for the government, but there you are."

Maisie didn't like to point out that Belladonna was probably just plain Donna from Brentville, who was knocking on fifty, with a husband, four children and a pet chinchilla.

"What do we do?" she said.

"I'm glad you asked me that," said Ramsey. "This is top detective stuff, you know. We need to break into the *Chronicle* files and look for clues."

"Isn't that illegal?" asked Maisie.

"Och aye, a little bit," said Ramsey. "But I'm a policeman. At least I used to be. And police are allowed to break the law."

Maisie didn't think that was completely true but she didn't say anything. It was too good a plan.

"Let's do it!" she said, feverish with excitement.

"Not yet," said Ramsey. "You've got school and I don't want you in any more bother than you already are. Come back here at half past three and we'll do it then."

"OK," said Maisie and she clutched Monkey Onassis tightly. She could hardly wait.

More Front Page News

At school all talk was of the biscuit scandal.

"I hear that if you eat an iced ring, your legs will fall off," said Lindy.

"That's nothing," said Mindy. "The really bad ones are the sponge fingers. Just one sniff and within minutes you're dead."

Only two people weren't joining in with the gossip. One was Maisie, who never told tales. The other was Belinda Braithwaite. She was sat on her own looking pale and quiet, which was very unusual for such a nasty bully.

"Cat got your tongue?" snapped Ms Bruton when she stamped into class.

Belinda shook her head.

"No – probably been burnt off by a rogue fig roll," said Ms Bruton meanly. "See – my NO BISCUIT rule paid off, didn't it? None of you horrible lot are

blue or dead, more's the pity. I shall think about adding NO DAUGHTERS OF POISONERS to the list though." And she smiled a horrible smile.

"But he's innocent," protested Belinda sadly.

"That's what they all say," snorted Ms Bruton.

"Don't listen to her," whispered Maisie to Belinda. "I believe you. And what's more, I'm going to find out what's really going on. Just you see."

Belinda looked at Maisie in shock. Then she said something she had never said before in her life.

"Thank you," she whispered back.

As soon as the school bell rang at half past three, Maisie ran out of the school gates, up Groutley High Street, past Dog About Town poodle parlour, past the Brentville bypass, up the long gravelly drive, in the front door – and straight into Mrs Morris, who was carrying a basket full of dirty laundry.

"Maisie Morris, you'll do yourself some terrible mischief if you keep on charging about like that," said Mrs Morris, picking a pair of giant underpants off the floor. "Where in the name of Jehosaphat are you going at that infernal speed anyway?"

"Ummm. I'm going to do some homework on Ramsey's computer," said Maisie. Which was almost true.

"Hmm. Well, just be careful with that thing," said Mrs Morris. "I don't trust computers. Apparently they're full of viruses and I don't want you catching something. You know what happened when Colonel Snell got the mumps."

"Yes, Ma," said Maisie. "Where's Monkey Onassis?"

"Last time I saw him he was in the rumpus room with a torch and a spanner, looking for interesting things behind the sofa. So who knows what manner of mess he's made or if the room hasn't been dismantled, flooded or blown to smithereens?"

Maisie flew up the turret stairs, grabbed Monkey Onassis from the rumpus room, where he had been unscrewing a large nut and bolt from the radiator, and burst through Ramsey's door.

"Just in time, lassie!" said Ramsey, smiling. "I was

about to start without you, I was so eager to be solving the mystery!" And he scooped Maisie up into his lap, who scooped Monkey Onassis up into hers so they were sitting in a little pyramid at the computer.

"Now, first of all we need to get into the *Chronicle*'s main compooter," said Ramsey.

"How will we do that?" asked Maisie.

"Just watch, lassie," said Ramsey and his long freckly fingers typed quickly on the keys. The screen went black for a second. Then it flashed red and the logo with the motto of the *Chronicle* – "Who Dares Wins" – appeared in the middle of screen and started spinning so ferociously it made Maisie's eyes go funny.

"Coo!" she said.

Ramsey hit some more keys.

"We're in!" he said.

And they were. At their fingertips were all the stories being typed up at that very minute by the reporters at the *Chronicle*.

There was one about the Groutley Ladies Benevolent Circle coffee morning being cancelled until further notice on account of the biscuit threat.

There was another one about some unsavoury

graffiti on the Bernard Gibbons Memorial Multi-Storey Car Park lift.

And there was yet another one about Mr Peason and his Cleethorpes Comet, which had won three rosettes and a Highly Commended at the Brentville Caravan Club Show.

"Nothing unusual there," said Ramsey. "Let's have a look at Lester's personal files." And he did some more fast typing.

A little box pinged up at the bottom of the screen marked TOP SECRET. On it was a picture of a skull and crossbones.

"That's got to be it," said Ramsey and clicked on it.

Another box appeared, asking him to type in his password.

"Hell and Dalmatians!" said Ramsey. "This is going to be tougher than I thought. Get your thinking-cap on, Maisie. We need to work out what Lester's password is."

First they tried the surnames of Lester's favourite football team, the Groutley Gunners (Grub, Grubb, Gribble, Jones, Nesbit, Oolong, Peabody, Perry, Wherry, Smith and Smee), then his mother's maiden name (Crabtree), and finally the name of his bull terrier (Kevin). None of them worked.

Then Maisie had an idea. She typed in L E S T E R.

It worked!

"Bingo!" shouted Ramsey. "How did you know?"

"Because he's so vain," said Maisie. "And stupid. He'd want something important to him and easy to remember."

"Well, let's see what he's cooking up at the moment," said Ramsey and he clicked on a file marked THURSDAY. A story flashed up with a headline as big and shouty as before.

"GROUTLEY GERIATRIC IS OUT OF THIS WORLD!" it read in triple-height letters. "*Pensioner Norman Armour is in league with aliens, it was revealed last night. The 87-year-old recluse has been plotting to take over the earth since 1953. The terrifying truth came to light after he was seen climbing into a flying saucer which had been hovering suspiciously over Groutley Rec just to the left of the adventure playground (disused). The extra-terrestrial craft then spun round several times before heading off in the night sky towards Nurding. Suspicions have been running high for months after eyewitness reports of Mr Armour talking covertly in corners with little green men.*"

"What eyewitness reports?" said Maisie. "I've never seen any aliens. The only little green people round here are the Groutley Scouts."

"This sounds fishy to me," said Ramsey. "Very fishy indeed. Come on, you two. Get your coats – we're going to pay someone a visit."

"Norman Armour?" asked Maisie.

Ramsey smiled. "The very same."

Norman Armour

Norman Armour was the most miserable man in Groutley. He still wore the same sludge-coloured cardigan his Aunt Maude had knitted him in 1937.

He lived a life of abstinence and austerity, eating canned pilchards and boiled vegetables, and only turning on his electric heater for a Christmas treat.

It was not that he didn't have any money, just that he didn't like to spend it.

He lived alone in a tiny terrace that had not changed since World War II, which was exactly how Norman liked it.

He had enjoyed the war immensely because his grommets meant he didn't have to go and fight Germans. Instead he got a job as a rations inspector and every day before blackout he stalked Groutley with a clipboard and pencil making sure no one was keeping illicit pigs or cheese or growing carrots in their coal cellar.

After the war ended and cheese was legal again, Norman took it upon himself to ride his rickety black bicycle round Groutley looking out for anyone breaking any by-laws. If he saw anything untoward, he wrote it down in his big leather-bound Misdemeanour Book.

If anyone hung overly fancy curtains in their drawing-room windows, or put their dustbins out a day early, their names would be blacklisted and sent to the council or complained about in long-winded letters to the *Groutley Chronicle* "Your Twopence Worth" page.

And woe betide any child playing ball in the street

or riding a bicycle on the pavement.

He didn't get paid for it. He just did it because he was cantankerous.

What was odd about Lester's story was that Norman did not believe in fairies, dwarves, elves, acupuncture or anything remotely out of the ordinary.

"So how can he be in league with something he doesn't think exists?" said Maisie as she reached up to knock on the door of 27 Arbuthnot Street.

After what seemed like an eternity, Maisie, Ramsey and Monkey Onassis heard footsteps clattering down the bare floorboards of the hallway. The door creaked open an inch and Norman Armour peered out. He had a long thin nose, grey skin and the look of someone who had sucked too hard on a lemon.

"What is it?" snapped Norman. "If you've lost a ball over my fence, then it's tough luck. I shall be reporting you for damaging my roses, and melting the ball down for emergency rubber supplies."

"You're still here!" exclaimed Maisie. "You're not with aliens!"

Norman looked down at her in disgust. "Of course I'm not with aliens. They don't exist, they've

been made up by the government to keep idiots like you occupied and stop you wondering what the government's really up to instead. Now kindly go away before I report you for trespassing." And he went to shut the door.

"No, please don't, Mr Armour," said Maisie, poking her foot into the hallway to stop the door closing. His house smelled of old things. "We need to talk to you urgently."

"There's something fishy afoot," added Ramsey.

"Poppycock!" said Norman. "You're just trying to worm your way into my very limited affections so that you can get in and steal my valuables."

"No, no, we're not," said Maisie. "We want to solve a mystery."

Norman looked closely at Maisie. "Wait a moment. I know who you are. You're Maisie Morris. You've come to check up on me so that your mother can cart me off to Withering Heights and sell my house for a tidy profit. Yes, that's it. Now get your foot off my threshold and off my property immediately, you interfering fiddle-faddlers. And I shall be reporting you for keeping a monkey without a licence as well." And he slammed the door in their faces, missing Maisie's toes by a hundredth of a millimetre.

"What do you think is going on?" asked Maisie.

"I'm not rightly sure," said Ramsey McDoon. "But I do know that we can't stay here all night – your ma will have my guts for garters. We'll just have to wait for tomorrow's paper. Then we'll know for sure if something's amiss."

Alien Invasion

Maisie and Monkey Onassis lay fast asleep in their beds in the titchy tiny turret, dreaming of ponies and fish fingers respectively, when they were awoken by an almighty banging on the door.

"Let me in!" shouted Ramsey. "It's here!"

Maisie jumped out of bed and opened the door to reveal Ramsey, frantically waving that morning's copy of the *Chronicle* in the air.

"Look at this!" he said, holding up the front page.

"Crikey!" said Maisie.

"Hoop!" said Monkey Onassis.

"My thoughts exactly," said Ramsey.

For there, in black and white, was the news that Norman Armour had indeed run away with aliens.

"So Lester really is up to no good!" said Maisie.

"That's right," said Ramsey. "I'm not sure exactly how he's doing it but I'd bet my last razoo on him making all these awful stories up and framing

innocent people, maybe even kidnapping them himself!"

"You mean he's lying?" asked Maisie.

"Absolutely!" said Ramsey, his eyes sparkling. "He's telling porkies, fibs, whoppers, claptrap and baloney!"

"But why would he do that?" asked Maisie.

"Because everyone loves a good horror story, Maisie," said Ramsey. "People are funny things. No one wants anything bad to happen to them but if it happens to someone else, they want to know every last rotten detail. And Lester is happy to give it to them, because the more hideous his stories, the more papers he sells and the richer he gets!"

"Gosh!" said Maisie. "That's terrible."

"Aye," said Ramsey. "But you've got to admit it's a cunning plan all right. Poison in your biscuits and aliens in your back garden – it's everyone's worst nightmare."

As if on cue, Mrs Morris came charging up the turret stairs, looking as white as a sheet and clasping her hands to her face.

"Aliens!" she screamed. "Barbara's been on the phone again. It's front-page news. We're being invaded by little green men who are going to enslave us and make us wear silver foil costumes and fly about in pods!"

"You mean *this*," said Maisie and held up the paper.

"Aaaghh!" shrieked Mrs Morris again. "That's it. Barbara says her sister-in-law Marjory saw one in the queue at Fishcoteque last night. They're everywhere. There's probably a whole herd of them hiding in my airing cupboard. I've always had my suspicions about Mr Armour. It's the quiet ones you have to watch. And the ones with shifty eyes. Or facial hair – men with beards or moustaches or those big sideboardy things have always got something to hide."

"But, Ma, it's not true," said Maisie. "Lester Sylvester made it up."

"Of course it's true. It's in the newspaper, isn't it?" said Mrs Morris. "The town's in chaos. The shops are selling out of loo roll and baked beans, and the schools have closed."

"But, Ma, we went to see Norman Armour last night—" began Maisie.

"Whaaat? Oh, my stars – you've probably been brainwashed by a giant probe from Mars and turned into an extra-territorial yourself!"

"No, I haven't, Ma," insisted Maisie.

"She's telling the truth," added Ramsey.

"I doubt it," said Mrs Morris.

"But—" began Ramsey.

"Not another word!" said Mrs Morris. "I've heard enough from you two to last me till teatime. Now, out of my way – Colonel Snell says he saw something suspicious in the downstairs toilet." And she pelted back down the stairs.

Maisie sighed. "Now what?" she said.

"There's only one thing for it," said Ramsey. "We'll have to go to the police."

PC Boggit

What with it being a fairly dull and small sort of place, Groutley only had one policeman and PC Boggit was it.

He was a short, stocky man with a round red face and an exceedingly stupid Alsatian called Arnie. Working in Groutley suited him down to the ground because the dullness and lack of crime meant he could spend his days eating doughnuts, watching detective shows on TV and reading magazines about fearful murders and how they were solved. So the recent turn of events had annoyed him immensely. Not only did he have two missing persons but the phone was ringing non-stop with reports of possible alien sightings.

PC Boggit was sitting at the front desk of Groutley Police Station eating a cherry Bakewell slice and reading a book called *Spacemen and How to Spot Them*

when Maisie, Ramsey and Monkey Onassis rang the bell for attention.

He peered over the page to see a giant ginger man in a kilt, a small blonde schoolgirl with particularly swoopy hair, and a monkey staring back at him.

"'Ello, 'ello, 'ello," he said. "What have we here then?"

"My name's Maisie Morris," said Maisie. "And I've got something important to tell you."

"Maisie Morris, is it?" said PC Boggit. "Well, well, well. I've heard all about you. You want to be more careful or you'll be in St Strangeway's by the age of ten. First it's trouble at school, then it's joyriding, then it's armed robbery before you can say 'Inspector Morse'. I've seen it happen time and time again."

"Who to?" said Maisie.

"Never you mind," said PC Boggit. "Nothing gets past me though. I've got eyes in the back of my head, an ear to the ground and fingers in every pie." Which, had it been true, would have looked very amusing indeed. However, the fact was that PC Boggit had yet to solve any crime whatsoever in Groutley. He preferred to watch it on telly, where they had better cars, better sunglasses and lots of beautiful ladies who always needed rescuing in the nick of time.

"We've come to tell you about the aliens," said Maisie.

"They don't exist," said Ramsey.

"Of course they exist," said PC Boggit, sighing. "It's in the paper. And who might you be anyway?"

"I'm Ramsey McDoon. Former Chief of Police on the glorious Kyle of Tongue."

"Really?" said PC Boggit, a little put out. "Well, I'm sure aliens didn't exist in the Isle of Wotsit, as there's nothing there but ginger cows and that horrible iron brew stuff; but Groutley's a bit more cosmopolitan than that and we're just the sort of place aliens would want to come to, if they fancied a trip to earth. There's the Hosepipe Museum, the Municipal Rose Gardens and the Groutley gyratory system, which is unique in Brentville Borough."

"Och, I'm not saying that aliens don't exist at all," said Ramsey. "Just that this lot doesn't."

"Lester Sylvester invented them," added Maisie. "Just like he made up the stuff about the poisonous biscuits."

124

"A likely story," said PC Boggit. "Anyway, I've had several calls already this morning about them. Mr Acropolis from Fishcoteque said that one ordered four super-saveloys and a pint of mushy peas, which no one on this planet would ever do. The vicar says someone's gone off with four bottles of Communion wine and a bumper box of those little wafery things. Stacey Flair from the bingo hall says a very small and suspicious-looking person got two full houses last night, which is unprecedented, and I've my own suspicions about who's behind the whole dog droppings scourge."

"But why would aliens scatter dog droppings around?" said Maisie. "And why would they steal wine and wafers?"

"Aha," said PC Boggit. "It'll be rocket fuel they're wanting it for."

"That's ridiculous," said Maisie. "And if you found Norman Armour, he'd tell you so himself."

"Aye," said Ramsey. "Have you not started hunting him down yet?"

"Right, that's enough," said PC Boggit. "First you come in here accusing a pillar of society like Lester Sylvester of fabricating evidence. Now you're questioning my detective skills. You had better skedaddle sharpish, the lot of you, or I shall arrest you for wasting police time." And he slammed the metal grille down over the window, just to show he meant business, and went back to his book and his cake.

"Well, if he won't look for Norman and Preston, then we'll have to do it ourselves," said Maisie as they walked home. "Then they'll have to believe us."

"By golly!" said Ramsey. "That's it. We must go on a manhunt. Och, this reminds me of the time I had to search for the Dread Pirate Finnegan out on the watery depths of Loch Ness with nothing but a torch and a piece of mint cake in my pocket."

"Did you find him?" asked Maisie.

"No," admitted Ramsey. "But I did catch a glimpse of Nessie herself! Although it could have been an exceptionally large eel. It was awful dark out there, you know."

126

Maisie smiled. "Come on then," she said. "We'd better start looking."

Back at Groutley Police Station, PC Boggit was thinking about Maisie Morris and her gang and the ridiculous story they had been telling him. Lester Sylvester was an acquaintance of his from the Groutley branch of the Triangular Table, which was a club for men only where they wore silly hats and talked in a special secret language (which had no point other than making all the members feel super important). But the top rule at the club was that the members had to help each other out whenever they could.

"I think I'll just give Lester a tinkle," said PC Boggit to Arnie, who was chasing his tail joyously around the room. "Warn him that his good name's in jeopardy."

And he picked up the phone and dialled Groutley 707.

Five minutes later, Lester put the phone down and swung round full circle on his chair.

"That meddling Morris is too clever for her own

good," he said to himself. "Well, I'll show her. No one messes with a champion cheat like me." And he laughed with the sort of menacing laugh that all villains have.

The Manhunt

Maisie, Ramsey and Monkey Onassis set off on a hunt to find Preston and Norman.

First of all they went to the biscuit factory. The gates were locked, the lights were out and the chimneys had stopped puffing out the sickly sweet biscuity smoke that usually clogged up Timbuktu Road.

"I don't think they can be here," said Maisie.

Next they went to Mr Armour's house, where they found several photographers and a coachload of science-fiction fans from Brentville but no Norman.

They searched the Scout hut on the Rec, where they found Mr Peabody, Mr Nidgett Junior and the Groutley First Troop busy making alien defences out of washing-up bottles and bits of string.

Then they searched the bicycle sheds behind St Regina's Primary, where, much to Maisie's horror, they found Ms Bruton checking for evidence of alien activity.

"What do you think you're doing, you horrible little hoodlum?"

"Nothing, Ms Bruton," said Maisie.

"I doubt that. You are always up to something, and if I find out what it is, then I shall punish you in ways so devious and new that I haven't even invented them yet."

"Gosh, she's not very kindly, is she?" said Ramsey when they'd left.

"No," said Maisie, "she's not."

130

Finally, they searched the alleyway behind Bingorama bingo hall, where they found Stacey Flair's spare toupee and a kazoo, which Monkey Onassis kept for later because he like the buzzy sound and the way it made his mouth tingle.

But Norman Armour and Preston Braithwaite were nowhere to be seen.

"This is hopeless," said Maisie as she and Ramsey sat down on a bench next to the children's playground. "We've been out all day and we haven't found either of them."

"Aye," said Ramsey. "My old detective nose must not be as strong as it used to be. I tell you what, let's go home and have some tea and then we can think about some more places they might have been hidden in. And we'd better check Lester's files on the compooter as well – see what will be on the front page tomorrow."

"OK," said Maisie and swung herself down off the bench. "Come along, Monkey Onassis." And she looked around to where he had been sitting. Her stomach lurched. He wasn't there any more. "Monkey Onassis?" she called. Then again, in a panicky voice. "MONKEY ONASSIS!"

Ramsey looked around but there was no sign of Monkey Onassis anywhere. Nothing was broken, nothing was being dug up and no one was screaming. The park was still.

"When did you last see him?" asked Ramsey.

"He was just there on the roundabout, playing the kazoo and wearing that wig from the bingo hall," said Maisie. "Where can he have gone?"

"Och, I'm sure he's just fine and dandy," said Ramsey, not wanting to worry Maisie. "He's probably already back at Withering Heights waiting for us. You know how easily he gets bored."

Maisie nodded. But something didn't feel right. She had an awful inkling he was in trouble. And although he didn't say anything to Maisie, Ramsey had the exact same inkling himself.

And the inklings were right.

Monkey Onassis and the Jewellery Heist

Maisie and Ramsey walked silently up Groutley High Street towards Withering Heights. Ramsey was chewing a Highland Toffee, so his teeth were a bit stuck together, and Maisie was too busy thinking about where Monkey Onassis might be to talk.

They were halfway up William Hague Way when PC Boggit's black maria shot past them with its siren blaring and Arnie the Alsatian's head sticking out of the passenger window, his tongue lolling sideways.

A few seconds later, the *Groutley Chronicle* van screeched round the corner in hot pursuit and disappeared up the road in a cloud of exhaust.

"Quick!" said Maisie. "Something's happened."

"By golly," said Ramsey. "What on earth can it be?"

They ran pell-mell up the road, through the great iron gates of Withering Heights, down the long gravelly drive, where the black maria and the *Groutley Chronicle* van were parked, and straight through the front door, where they were greeted by Mrs Morris, whose eyes were on stalks and whose hair looked as if someone had plugged her into a wall socket.

"Maisie Morris!" she shrieked. "Where the devil have you been? That flaming monkey of yours has really done it this time."

Maisie's tummy lurched again. She knew it — something awful had happened. She looked round her ma into the hallway. There were PC Boggit and Arnie, Lester Sylvester holding a reporter's notebook, and all the residents of Withering Heights looking over the banisters at the excitement below.

And in the middle of it all was Monkey Onassis, sitting on the floor still wearing the toupee and holding his kazoo but looking very confused and a little sorry for himself.

"Oh, Monkey Onassis!" said Maisie, running up to

him and flinging her arms round his neck. "What's happened? Where did you get to?"

"I'll tell you where he got to," shrieked Mrs Morris. "That flibbertigibbet has only gone and robbed Van Spangle's Jeweller's of several hundred thousand pounds' worth of diamonds."

Maisie looked at her in horror. "But he can't have!" she said. "He was with us nearly all day."

"*Nearly* all," said PC Boggit, stepping forward and eyeing Maisie with a self-satisfied sort of look. "But not *all* day, because at some point he managed to break through several security devices, including the latest sophisticated alarm system, a ferocious guard dog and a trip wire, and steal a set of ruby earrings and a diamond-encrusted eggcup."

"Rubbish!" said Ramsey.

"Alas not," said PC Boggit. "I've found the evidence in his hairy paw." And he held up the ruby earrings, which lit up the hallway with a red glow and made it look like the set of a horror film.

"What about the eggcup?" said Ramsey.

"He must have stashed it on his way back here,"

explained PC Boggit. "Don't worry, we'll find it eventually."

"Someone must have planted the rubies on him," said Maisie. "He didn't do it himself. He couldn't have."

"Oh, but there's witnesses," said Lester.

"What are you doing here?" said Maisie.

"Covering the story, of course," said Lester with a greasy smile. "It's front-page stuff this."

"Who saw him then?" asked Maisie indignantly.

"Oh, I can't reveal my sources," said Lester, and he laughed nastily. "First rule of journalism, that."

"He fitted the description exactly," added PC Boggit. "Even down to the disguise." And he pointed to Monkey Onassis's ginger toupee.

Maisie shook her head in disbelief. This couldn't be happening.

"We believe he could be working for the notorious Nutmeg Gang," said PC Boggit. "We're linking him to a spate of robberies across the borough."

"But he doesn't know any Nutmeg Gang," said Maisie. "And he doesn't steal things any more."

"Really?" said Lester, turning to Mrs Morris and flicking through the pages of his notebook. "Mrs Morris, did you or did you not say these very words to me in my office two days ago: 'He's probably wanted dead or alive for all those wretched diamonds he stole... He's a terror for the gems.'"

"Cripes, I did say that," she replied. "You've got a good memory."

"But, Ma," said Maisie, "Monkey Onassis didn't steal anything. I know he didn't. Lester's lying. Just like he lied about Preston Braithwaite and Norman Armour."

"Preposterous!" snorted Lester.

"Oh, duck, I know you love that monkey, but if he's been bad, then he has to go to prison," said Mrs Morris. "Heaven knows it would be quieter round here anyway – which would be a nice change."

"Maybe Maisie's in on it all as well," said Lester. "Maybe she's the criminal mastermind behind it all."

"No, I'm not," said Maisie. "I didn't do anything."

"Very well then," said PC Boggit. "I'll just take the monkey. Let's be having the fellow." And he opened the door to a large metal birdcage that had previously belonged to his mother's pet parrot, Percy, and that he had kept in a cupboard in case it came in useful one day. Which it just had.

"No!" wailed Maisie.

But it was too late. With only a minor scuffle, and some spitting on the part of Monkey Onassis, he was behind bars.

"Right. That's it," said PC Boggit. "Move along now. Nothing to see here."

"Oh, Monkey Onassis!" cried Maisie.

"Hoop!" shrieked Monkey Onassis through the cage, not knowing where he was going but certain that wherever it was, it wouldn't involve toast or fish fingers or Maisie.

"Oh, stop – you're upsetting him!" sobbed Maisie. But he was gone.

Maisie sat down on the stairs, tears rolling down her pale cheeks onto her cardigan. She had lost her reputation and now, even worse, she had lost Monkey Onassis.

She had to get them back. And she had to do it soon.

"Hush now, luvvie," said Mrs Morris. "I'll make you some nice cocoa and it'll all be better by tomorrow morning. You'll see."

But Maisie wasn't so sure.

The New Plan

As Maisie had thought, Mrs Morris was wrong. The next morning, nothing was better. In fact, it was worse.

Monkey Onassis was on the front page of the *Chronicle*, just as Lester had promised.

"MONKEY BUSINESS!" it proclaimed. "*International jewel thief Monkey Onassis is back behind bars this morning after a daring but ill-fated raid on top Groutley gem superstore Van Spangle's Jeweller's. The simian sneak was caught red-pawed at his hideout in Withering Heights Retirement Home with two ruby earrings about his person. A priceless diamond-encrusted eggcup is still missing and Clint Van Spangle himself is offering a £50 reward for any information leading to its safe return.*"

"This is terrible," said Maisie as she sat on the end of Ramsey's bed, still pale and wet from all the crying. "It's all our fault. We should have been

checking Lester's computer instead of looking for Preston and Norman. Now Monkey Onassis is probably being tortured and interrogated – or eaten by that enormous Alsatian."

In fact, Monkey Onassis was not having too bad a time. He'd had a boiled egg for breakfast and was now spending an enjoyable hour jumping up at the bars on his cell door, taunting the daft and hopeless Arnie, who in turn kept jumping up at the door, banging his head on the handle, yelping in pain every time he did so.

But in Maisie's vivid imagination Monkey Onassis was being handcuffed and thrown into a dungeon. She had to get him out of there. But how, she didn't know.

"Lester Sylvester framed him. I just know it," she said. "Just like he framed Preston Braithwaite and Norman Armour. But no one will believe us, because we don't have any evidence."

Ramsey looked at her. "By jingo, you've got it!"

"Got what?" said Maisie morosely.

"Evidence," said Ramsey. "That's what we need. We need to catch Lester red-handed. Then we'll have all the proof PC Boggit needs."

"What do you mean?" asked Maisie. "We can't

catch Lester. He's far too clever."

"We can if we use the right bait," said Ramsey. "He may be clever. But you, Maisie Morris, are a good deal cleverer. Now think. What does Lester like best?"

Maisie smiled weakly. "Horrible stories," she said.

"Right first time!" said Ramsey. "So all we have to do is think up a horrible story for him and then catch him trying to carry it out."

"But why would he want to print our story?" said Maisie. "He could just make up one of his own."

"Because ours will be the most horrible, ghastly story you could imagine. It will be so frightening it will make small children hide behind the sofa when they hear about it," said Ramsey.

Maisie thought hard about the sort of ghoulish stories Lester Sylvester would like. Maybe one of Ramsey's famous boggarts terrorizing Brownie Revels. Maybe the whole town being trampled on by a leftover Tyrannosaurus rex who'd been hiding in the portable toilets at Razzmatazz Roller Rink.

Then she got it.

"Me," she said.

Ramsey looked puzzled. "What do you mean, lass?" he asked, stroking his beard quizzically.

"I mean he'd like a horrible story about me," she said. "That's it. That's what we'll do!" And she smiled a big wide Maisie smile.

"Tell me more," said Ramsey.

"We'll write the most gruesome story possible about me. Then we'll give it to him," said Maisie. "We'll tell him he can carry out the story to the last detail as long as he tells us the truth about Monkey Onassis."

"But, Maisie!" said Ramsey, leaping around the room in terror. "I don't want to see you mangled or mown down or chopped up for dog food."

"Yuck!" said Maisie. "Anyway, I won't be, silly. Because later on, when he tries to carry out the last detail, we'll catch him red-handed. Or at least PC Boggit will!"

Ramsey stopped jumping about and looked at Maisie. "Of course!" he said. "Sorry, I was so worried, I forgot my own plan."

"That's OK," said Maisie. "But we have to get to work. First of all we need to write the story on your computer – straight into Lester's top secret file so he knows we mean business. It has to be nasty and violent and unimaginably awful."

"Very well," said Ramsey. "Let's start typing."

And it *was* awful. So awful that I'm afraid your eyes might pop out if I tell you what happens to Maisie. But then, I'll have to take that risk, or we'll get stuck at this point in the story and that would be tricky.

This is what it said: "GROUTLEY GIRL IN KIDNAP HORROR. *Eight-year-old Maisie Morris is missing this morning after being kidnapped by a child-snatcher called Erno Cragg at 7.00 p.m. last night. Police were alerted after a passer-by discovered Morris's right ear and little fingers on a bench in Groutley Rec at 7.05 p.m. They were Sellotaped to a ransom note which demanded £1,000 by the end of the week, or more of little Maisie's fingers and ears are going to be chopped off. Mrs Morris, Maisie's mother, was too distraught for comment, but her friend Ramsey McDoon had this to say: 'Och, it's a rotten shame. After her pet monkey was released from prison as well because he didn't steal those jewels after all.' Anyone with information or donations should call kind-hearted Lester Sylvester at the* Chronicle, *who is in charge of the campaign to bring little Maisie back."*

"Brilliant!" said Ramsey when Maisie had finished.

"Not too horrible?" said Maisie.

"Och no. Just right," said Ramsey. "Lester will lap it up. But who's Erno Cragg?"

"I made him up," said Maisie.

"Excellent!" said Ramsey. "Now, what's next?"

"Next we phone Lester and tell him about our arrangement," said Maisie.

"Hurrah!" shouted Ramsey and punched his fist into the air.

"Hello, Ma," said Maisie as she and Ramsey hopped excitedly into the kitchen. "Can we use the phone?"

"Oooh, morning, Maisie," said Mrs Morris, clattering breakfast plates noisily. "I thought you'd be moping about after that flaming monkey of yours. Honest to goodness, Maisie, you know I love you,

146

but that creature is more trouble than he's worth."

"No, he's not, Ma. I love him," said Maisie. "And I haven't forgotten him, I'm going to see him later when they set him free."

"Oh, Maisie," said Mrs Morris, and she sighed. "You have to give up, luvvie. He's more guilty than a small boy with an empty sweet packet. They'll have thrown the key away by now."

"Well, they'll jolly well have to find it again," said Maisie. "Because I'll never give up. And please can I use the phone?"

"Who are you calling?" asked Mrs Morris suspiciously. "Not that monkey, I hope, because prisoners aren't allowed phone calls, and besides, you know how he likes to chew telephone wire."

"No, Ma," said Maisie. "I promise."

"Go on then," said Mrs Morris. "But don't be long. I want to call Barbara to tell her all the frightful details about last night."

"Thanks, Ma," said Maisie and disappeared into the hallway with Ramsey to make the call.

The Arrangement

Lester was spinning around on his leather chair, smoking a celebratory cigarette and thinking about how cunningly he'd framed Monkey Onassis when the phone rang.

"What?" he thundered into the receiver.

"Mr Sylvester?" said a small voice.

"Who wants to know?" barked Lester.

"It's Maisie Morris, sir," said Maisie.

"Morris, is it?" Lester smiled to himself. "Well, well, well. What can I do for you? Missing your little monkey friend, are you?"

Maisie clenched her hand so tightly around the receiver that her knuckles turned white.

"Don't stop now," whispered Ramsey. "You can do it."

Maisie swallowed and took a big breath. "I've got a deal for you," she said.

"A deal indeed?" scoffed Lester. "And what makes

 you think I'll do business with you?"

"We know all about how you make up the stories to sell newspapers," said Maisie. "So we've made one up for you. But if you print it, you have to promise to tell us the truth about Monkey Onassis."

"I don't know what you're talking about," lied Lester.

Ramsey, who was listening in over Maisie's shoulder, grabbed the phone.

"Now, you listen to me, Jim lad," he said boldly. "I know and you know that Monkey Onassis did not steal the diamonds, and you know that I know that you know who did."

"First of all, my name's not Jim," snapped Lester. "And secondly, who on earth are you?"

"I'm Ramsey McDoon. Former Chief of Police on the glorious Kyle of Tongue and current friend of the glorious Maisie Morris."

Lester thought to himself. He did not want to admit anything about the jewellery heist. On the other hand, he was intrigued by the offer.

"Go on then, McDoon," he said slyly into the phone. "What's the story?"

"We've got him!" whispered Ramsey gleefully to Maisie, and he let her take the phone again.

"Hello, Mr Sylvester," she said.

"Oh, it's you again," said Lester. "Well, come on then. What's this story that's so exciting I'll be putting it on my front page?"

"It's in your secret computer file," said Maisie. "Under SATURDAY. Just click on it and you'll see."

Lester's face turned a very angry shade of red. "What do you mean it's in my file? How did you get in there, you sneak?"

"Never mind that now," said Maisie. "Just look at it. I think you'll like it."

Lester dropped the phone receiver onto the table, making a nasty clattering sound right into Maisie's ear, and tapped something into the computer.

"Well, I'll be hanged," he said. Because sure enough, there it was, and it was more gruesome and filthy than even Lester could ever have imagined.

"She's even stupider than I thought," Lester said to himself. "She's going to sacrifice herself just to save that horrible, hairy monkey." And he smiled a nasty smile and picked the phone up again.

"Very well," he said. "I'll see you at the Bandstand at seven o'clock sharp. I'll tell you about Monkey Onassis then."

"OK," said Maisie and hung up the phone. Then she hugged Ramsey. "We've done it!" she cried.

"Hold your horses there, lassie," said Ramsey, putting her back on her feet. "There's still a lot of work to be done before we can say that. You've got to think of an excuse to tell your ma so she'll let you out of the house tonight. And I've got to persuade PC Boggit to be at the scene on time. And that could take some mighty strong persuading indeed."

But Maisie's spirits couldn't be dampened. Nothing could stop her now. She was going to get Monkey Onassis back and save Preston Braithwaite and Norman Armour and get Lester Sylvester arrested.

Wasn't she?

The Excuse

"Maisie Morris, where do you think you're going dressed like that?" said Mrs Morris as Maisie came down the stairs after supper. "You know yellow and brown aren't your colours – Barbara says you should wear more blue, with your hair."

"It's my Brownie uniform," said Maisie. Which was true. "I'm going to do a good deed on Groutley Rec."

"Oh, so it is," said Mrs Morris. "Well, mind you keep together with all the other little Brownies. I don't want you getting mistaken for aliens and being gunned down by PC Boggit and his horde of armed officers."

"I don't think that's likely to happen," said Maisie. "Anyway, Ramsey is coming with me."

"That I am," added Ramsey, who was dressed in his kilt and official Chief of Police's ceremonial Tam o' Shanter.

"Lor' love a duck," said Mrs Morris. "You two are a

right pair in your outfits. Well, you be good and enjoy yourselves but I want her back by half past seven sharp, Mr McDoon. Is that understood?"

"Aye, Mrs Morris," said Ramsey.

"Hmm," said Mrs Morris. "Why do I get a funny feeling in my feet that you two are hatching something?"

"Oh, that'll be your slippers," said Ramsey. "I expect Monkey Onassis left some itching powder in them."

Mrs Morris looked down. "Yes, well, I wouldn't put anything past that varmint. It's a good thing he's locked up or I'd shut him up myself in that tin of his." And she stamped off up the hallway to dust down her slippers.

"This is it, Maisie," said Ramsey. "This is the beginning of the end for Lester Sylvester."

"Then let's get started," said Maisie.

And so they did.

They walked down William Hague Way and turned left onto Groutley High Street. They walked past Totally Trousers with its window display of gigantic dungarees, past Fishcoteque with its long queue of hungry teenagers, past the *Chronicle* offices with their rows of frantic reporters typing furiously, and down to the turning for the Razzmatazz Roller Rink, where they stopped and Ramsey crouched down so that he could see eye to eye with Maisie.

"This is where we go our separate ways," he said. "Will you be OK?"

"Of course," said Maisie. "Because I know you'll be there as soon as you've told PC Boggit what's going on."

"That's right," said Ramsey. "So just be brave and don't let Lester scare you."

"I won't," said Maisie. "I promise."

"Good girl," said Ramsey and he hugged her tight so that his beard tickled her cheeks.

"Just think," said Maisie. "In an hour Monkey Onassis will be free and Lester will be behind bars."

Ramsey laughed. "Go on then, lass. No time to waste." And he stood up so that he towered above her again.

156

"Goodbye," he said.

"Goodbye," said Maisie.

And they turned around and walked in opposite directions: Maisie to meet Lester at Groutley Rec; and Ramsey to the Police Station to persuade PC Boggit to come to the scene.

The Kidnap

Groutley Rec was dark and cold. Maisie sat on the same roundabout that Monkey Onassis had been playing on when he went missing and spun round slowly, shivering in her Brownie uniform, partly from the cold and partly because she was scared.

She began to wish several things. Firstly, that she had had the good sense to wear her duffel coat. Secondly, that she had brought a torch with her. And thirdly, that she hadn't added the gruesome details about the ear and fingers being chopped off. But then she reminded herself that nothing bad was going to happen anyway because Ramsey and PC Boggit would be arriving very soon indeed.

She looked at her second-hand watch with the slightly cracked glass that Mrs Morris had given her for Christmas. It told her it was quarter to seven – not long to go until Lester arrived.

"Oh, hurry up and get it over with," said Maisie out loud.

At that very moment something thudded onto the roundabout behind her. Then Maisie felt something warm on the back of her neck. There was a sort of slow, heavy panting noise and a stale smell like Mr Nidgett after he'd smoked a cigar at Christmas.

Maisie gulped. Maybe it was an alien after all. Maybe Lester had been telling the truth. Maybe she was about to get transported to Jupiter any second.

But then the creature spoke.

"Hello, treacle," it said.

Maisie turned round. "Lester!" she said. "You're early."

"Of course," said Lester and smiled, showing his nasty yellow teeth which glowed in the dark. "I've been looking forward to this."

He looked her up and down.

"Like the uniform," he said. "Nice touch. That will come up a treat on the front-page photo."

Maisie didn't say anything. But Lester didn't care – he was too excited.

"I can't tell you how delighted I am we're going to be doing business together," he said, rubbing his hands together in delight. "Of course, I'm not the only one who'll benefit. You are going to be famous up and down the land after this. Do you want to see?"

Maisie nodded warily.

Lester reached inside his dirty macintosh and pulled out a large piece of paper, which he unfurled and held up in the moonlight. It was the front page of tomorrow's *Chronicle* – all about Maisie.

"Wonderful, isn't it?" said Lester. "A stroke of genius. The story will run for days as people become desperate to find out who killed little Maisie Morris. Imagine it: a double-page spread with celebrity interviews; her mother mourning at the graveside. Oh, the dignity of it all. It's a guaranteed bestseller."

But something wasn't right. The story was similar to the one Maisie had written. But it wasn't exactly the same. Lester had changed some of the details. Some

161

of the very important details like what happened to Maisie where and at what time.

"But that's not it!" said Maisie. "That's not the story I wrote."

"I know," said Lester. "It's better. Instead of being kidnapped, you get tied to the railway track and run over by the seven twenty-one Brentville-to-Sudbury Express."

"But you can't do that!" said Maisie.

"Why not?" said Lester. "You didn't think I'd stick to your version, did you? Why, it could have been a trick all along. I could have been ambushed." And he smiled a knowing smile. "Now, come along, we've got news to make."

And he clapped his fat, hairy hand over Maisie's mouth so she couldn't scream, grabbed her around the waist, jumped off the roundabout and carried her off towards Groutley Station.

The Great Persuasion of PC Boggit

Meanwhile, less than half a mile away, Ramsey McDoon had just rung the bell at Groutley Police Station.

PC Boggit, who was in the tea room watching his favourite episode of *Cops in Socks* – a show about two top detectives who solved all their crimes wearing bright argyle socks – gave an enormous huff of annoyance and stamped down the corridor.

"Oh, it's you, is it?" he said when he saw Ramsey. "I suppose you've come to see Monkey Onassis, have you? Well, tough! He's lost all visiting privileges after he tried to dig his way out of the cell with his dinner fork. A right old mess he's made of that lino – which, no doubt, *I'll* get the blame for when the County Chief comes to visit. And he's upset Arnie that much I'm adding 'cruelty to animals' to the list of charges against him. Which means he won't be out of prison until he's 104."

Unfortunately for PC Boggit, Monkey Onassis had misbehaved quite spectacularly, due to the fact that he was getting more and more annoyed.

Firstly, he missed Maisie enormously. He missed the way she brushed his fur until it shone like a conker. He missed the way she read him stories from her *Bumper Book of Fairy Tales* every night before bed. And he missed the way she let him eat her fish fingers even when she really wanted them for herself.

Secondly, he was bored. Cells are very spartan affairs with few cracks and crannies and thus precious few places to hide diamonds, which was what Monkey Onassis liked to do when he had nothing else pressing.

All this agitation combined meant he was more than usually destructive and had so far managed to break four dinner plates, dismantle the bed and give Arnie an enormous bruise on his head where he kept hitting it on the cell door handle.

"No, I've not come for him. Although I expect I'll be seeing him walk out of here a free monkey later on when you hear what I've got to say."

PC Boggit gave Ramsey one of his hard stares which he had learned from *Cops in Socks*.

"Now, you listen here, you ginger weirdo. I will not have you telling me how to do my job. I have made that clear. The monkey's guilty and that's all there is to it."

But Ramsey was not going to be put off by PC Boggit's tough cop routine and leaned forward over the desk in a purposeful manner.

"Get your notepad out, Boggit," he said. "I am reporting a crime, and by law you have to take down details."

PC Boggit knew this was true but he still harumphed a bit for effect before slapping a piece of paper down on the desk.

"Go on then. What is it?" he said, trying to sound bored.

"Now, this is important," said Ramsey. "The details are precise. Tonight, at seven o'clock exactly, Lester Sylvester is going to kidnap Maisie Morris from Groutley Rec. And you, PC Boggit, are going to be there to stop him."

PC Boggit looked at his wristwatch. He had got it in the post that morning from a special police gadget catalogue. It told the time in Tokyo, New York and Brussels and had a secret compartment for storing cough lozenges. It was thirteen minutes to seven.

"But that's ridiculous, McDoon," he said. "You can't report a crime before it happens."

"I can and I have," said Ramsey defiantly. "And do you want to know how I know this is going to happen? Because it's on the front page of tomorrow's *Chronicle*. And if you don't believe me, you can check the files yourself."

"What *are* you talking about?" flustered PC Boggit. "How do you know what's in tomorrow's papers? It's impossible."

"Take a look for yourself if you don't believe me. Here – these are the instructions." And he took a piece of paper out of his sporran and handed it to PC Boggit.

"This is gobbledygook," said PC Boggit, looking at Ramsey's scribbles. "I can't work from this. I'm a professional."

"Professional? Hah!" scoffed Ramsey. "I'm clearly a

far better detective than you."

"No, you're not," said PC Boggit.

"Yes, I am."

"No, you're not."

"Yes, I am... Look, we haven't got time for this. Here, I'm coming in." And Ramsey swung his big hairy legs over the desk.

"Stop! You're not allowed to do that!" said PC Boggit. "This is against all police regulations. I'll have you charged with trespass and criminal damage and impersonating a police officer."

"Oh, shut up, Boggit!" said Ramsey. "Look!" And he tapped away at PC Boggit's computer.

Within seconds he had bypassed the *Chronicle* logo, which was still spinning ferociously around the screen, and had found the file for Saturday's paper.

"There you are," he said and turned the screen round so that PC Boggit could see.

PC Boggit looked. Then he looked again just to make sure.

Then his face turned pale and his moustache wilted visibly.

"Well, blow me down with a feather," he said. "You're right. You've been right all along. Lester Sylvester is up to no good."

"Exactly," said Ramsey triumphantly. "And he's been up to it for days. The poisoned biscuits, the aliens (which don't exist), the stolen jewellery, they're all down to him."

"By gum!" said PC Boggit. "He had me fooled all right. He was the one who called the police every time to report the crime."

Ramsey smiled. "You've cracked it!"

PC Boggit beamed. "We make a top detective team, you and me," he said. "We could have our own show: *Boggit and McDoon.* Got a nice ring to it, hasn't it?

"Och aye," said Ramsey. "But we've got to stop the crime first. Come on – we've only got a few minutes to get to the scene!"

"Right you are!" said PC Boggit. "Come on, Arnie."

Arnie jumped for joy, his tongue dripping drool everywhere.

"What about Monkey Onassis?" said Ramsey. "Shouldn't we take him as well? He is innocent after all."

"Of course," said PC Boggit. "The more the merrier."

And so, with Ramsey in the front and Arnie and a joyous Monkey Onassis in the back, PC Boggit sped off towards Groutley Rec in his black maria.

Hurrah! I can hear you thinking. But then I can hear you thinking something else as well, something rather awful: why is he heading to Groutley Rec when Maisie is at this moment being tied to the train track at Groutley Station ready to be flattened by the seven twenty-one Brentville-to-Sudbury Express?

Ah. You're right! PC Boggit and Ramsey were so excited they didn't bother to read the whole story on the computer and see that Lester had made some rather horrible changes.

Well, that's it! I hear you cry. Maisie's number is up; her goose is cooked; she's as dead as a dodo! Lester is going to have her run over while PC Boggit and Ramsey are on the wrong side of town entirely.

Aha! But haven't you forgotten someone else? Someone small and hairy, with a nose for mystery?

Arnie?

No. Monkey Onassis, of course. I am sure he won't let anything happen to Maisie. So let's just wait and see...

Monkey Onassis's Nose

At 6.59 p.m. PC Boggit, Ramsey, Arnie and Monkey Onassis screeched to a halt on the Groutley Rec car park and bundled out of the black maria towards the playground.

"Where is she?" said PC Boggit.

Ramsey looked around wildly. "I don't know – she's supposed to be here."

But the park was deserted. The only sounds were the crisp packets rustling in the flowerbeds and the squeak of the roundabout slowly coming to a halt.

"I hope you've not been having me on," said PC Boggit, suddenly getting cold feet about the whole escapade. "This had better not be a trick to get the monkey out of jail."

"It's not," said Ramsey and his eyes began to fill with tears which shone wetly in the night.

172

PC Boggit saw them and knew he was telling the truth.

Then they heard a funny noise in the bushes and a short figure loomed out at them.

"Maisie?" cried Ramsey.

"No, it jolly well isn't," said the figure. "Although where she is I would like to know. All that claptrap about the Brownies – Barbara says that Brownies has been cancelled on account of the alien threat, so if it's cancelled, what's Maisie doing on Groutley Rec at this time of night and why aren't you with her, Mr McDoon, and why is that flaming monkey out of prison?"

"Mrs Morris?" said Ramsey.

"Of course it is," said Mrs Morris.

"Oh dear," said Ramsey. "Something terrible has happened."

"I knew it!" shrieked Mrs Morris. "She is an alien after all. She's been beamed up to join Norman Armour on his interplanetary mission from Mars."

"No, she hasn't," said PC Boggit. "Aliens don't exist. Everyone knows that."

Mrs Morris glared at him. "Well, where is she then?"

"She's been kidnapped," said Ramsey.

"By Lester Sylvester," added PC Boggit. "And he's going to chop her ears and fingers off if we don't find her right away."

"Oh, my stars!" she wailed. "What am I going to do? My precious Maisie! How could you let this happen?" And she began hitting Ramsey with her washing-up brush which she always carried with her in case of cleaning emergencies.

But while Ramsey, PC Boggit and Mrs Morris were arguing, Monkey Onassis had slid away from them and climbed up onto the roundabout. He knew that Maisie was in trouble and that he alone could find her. And there was only one way to do that. Monkey Onassis looked up into the night sky and sniffed the air long and hard.

174

Monkey Onassis worked by smell and he was good at it – he could smell a gleaming diamond across a desert. But tonight what he could smell wasn't diamonds. It was something far rarer and more precious. It was Maisie.

He let out a long low "hoop", which echoed around the park and sounded like a hundred Monkey Onassises all crying together.

"What's that?" said PC Boggit.

"It's Monkey Onassis," said Ramsey. "I think he's found something."

But before they had a chance to ask him what it was, he was off! Past Mr Majoob's kiosk which sold ice creams and toffees and strawberry shoelaces, past the skateboard park, where bigger boys spun in the air and skated on their hands, annoying old ladies who thought it was far too dangerous, past the Scout hut with its new alien defences and out of Groutley Rec towards Groutley Station.

"Follow that monkey!" shouted PC Boggit. And he jumped into his black maria with Ramsey and Mrs Morris and Arnie all crammed in the back and set off in hot pursuit.

Groutley Station

"Ow!" cried Maisie. "You're hurting me."

"Well, it has to be tight or you could wriggle away before the train gets here," sneered Lester, giving the rope he was using to tie Maisie down a good hard yank.

"Ow!" said Maisie again.

"Shut up, or I'll gag you as well," snapped Lester.

He looked at his watch. "Seventeen minutes past seven," he said. "Let's hope the Express is running on time." And he looked up the tracks towards Brentville. "Of course, at first you won't hear the train. You'll just feel the sleepers vibrate so that the bones in your back tingle," he said nastily. "As the train gets nearer, they'll start to shake harder and you'll be able to hear it in the distance. *Clickety-clack. Clickety-clack.* Then, when you hear it whistle, you had better shut your eyes and say your prayers, because any

177

second ... *splat!* You'll be as dead as that fly."

"What fly?" said Maisie.

"That one," said Lester and he slammed his hand down on a bluebottle which had been sitting happily on a rail, minding its own business.

Maisie winced, which made the ropes tighten around her even more. This was terrible. Having your ears and fingers chopped off was nothing compared to this. It was true: no one could outwit a liar like Lester. She should never have tried. She should have done as Ms Bruton told her – be seen and not heard.

She thought of her poor ma, having to scrape her up off the tracks with her dustpan and brush. And Ramsey, who'd get the biggest shouting-at ever. And poor, poor Monkey Onassis in prison for ever with just stale bread and water, his feet in chains.

A tear rolled out of her left eye and plopped onto the rail.

"Any minute now," said Lester. "Can you feel it yet?"

Maisie lay still. She could feel something. Something rumbling in the distance.

"Oh, crikey!" she said.

178

It was coming nearer. But it didn't sound like she'd expected. Instead of a *clickety-clack* it was more like the wail of a police siren mixed in with something that sounded very much like...

"Monkey Onassis!" cried Maisie.

And it was. He jumped off platform one and flew through the air, landing on Maisie's chest.

She tried to throw her arms around him, but they were tied down.

"Oh, Monkey Onassis, I thought you were locked up for ever. I have missed you so much."

"Hoop!" said Monkey Onassis as he buried his head into her neck. He would have cried for joy if monkeys had tears.

"What the devil is he doing here?" said Lester.

"There they are!" said a voice.

Maisie turned her head on the rail. She could just see some black shoes and a pair of bare, hairy legs striding towards her.

"Ramsey!" she cried.

"The very same, lassie, the very same," he said as he knelt down next to her.

"What are you doing, you meddling man?" snapped Lester. "You agreed to this as part of our business."

"We agreed to nothing, Lester. You lied, which makes anything we said null and void," said Ramsey.

He reached into his sporran, pulled out a long curved knife like a cutlass and with one swift movement sliced through the ropes that were holding Maisie down.

Then he picked her and Monkey Onassis up in his arms and lifted them to the safety of platform one, where Mrs Morris was waiting, while PC Boggit used the same rope to tie Lester up in a super-strong knot.

"Oh, my giddy aunt, you're alive!" cried Mrs Morris, hugging Maisie and Monkey Onassis so tightly they felt their eyes bulge out of their sockets. "I'll never doubt you again, my precious poppet.

And you too, Monkey Onassis. You can dismantle anything you want to and have fish fingers for tea for the rest of your life."

"Thanks, Ma," said Maisie and squeezed her back.

"And as for you, Lester Sylvester," said Mrs Morris. "What do you think you're doing trying to squish my little Maisie."

"What do you mean?" said Lester, scowling. "She could have been world famous and you could have sold your sob story for a fortune. A couple more minutes and the Brentville-to-Sudbury Express would have thundered through and made millionaires of us both."

"No, it wouldn't," said a croaky voice behind them.

Everyone turned round. It was Old Soames the station master, a short, white-haired man with long whiskery sideburns and a regulation cap.

"It was cancelled on account of all the hoo-ha in the papers. And what are you doing here anyway? Here's an old fellow trying to have forty winks in the ticket office when he gets disturbed for the third time this week. I tell you it's like Piccadilly Circus here."

"Why?" asked Maisie. "What else has happened?"

"Ooh, all sorts of comings and goings in the night with torches and things," said Old Soames. "And then there's those strange ghostly voices coming up from the old train shed arguing about chocolate digestives or summat like that. I 'spect it's them aliens hiding out."

"It's not aliens," said Maisie. "It's Preston Braithwaite!"

"And Norman Armour," added Ramsey.

"'Oo the devil are they?" asked Old Soames. "And what's more, what are they doing in my service shed?"

"Lester Sylvester kidnapped them and hid them here so they couldn't blab about his made-up stories," said Ramsey.

"Is it true, Lester?" said PC Boggit.

"Maybe," snapped Lester.

And it was. In the corner of the service shed, sitting in a disused carriage, was a dishevelled Preston Braithwaite, his hair no longer slicked back and his pinstriped suit covered in pigeon poo. Next to him, his face as thin and sour as week-old junket, sat Norman Armour.

"About time," said Preston Braithwaite, wresting a large and stupid woodpigeon off his shoulder.

184

"I shall be complaining in full to the Municipal Council about this," said Norman Armour. "And to the railway authorities. And to the RSPB."

"Hurrah!" said everyone.

"Fiddlesticks!" said Lester.

"Hang on," said Maisie. "The diamond heist. You said you'd tell us the truth about that too."

"Well, I lied," said Lester. "As far as I'm concerned, that nasty little monkey can get back behind bars where he belongs."

"But that's not fair!" said Maisie. She turned to PC Boggit. "You're not going to arrest him again, are you?"

"I'm sorry, Maisie," said PC Boggit, "but he was caught with the earrings on him and unless Lester confesses, there's no other explanation."

"Oh, Monkey Onassis!" cried Maisie.

But Monkey Onassis was not listening. He had something else on his mind. He put his nose in the air and sniffed again.

"What's he doing?" asked PC Boggit.

"I'll tell you what he's doing – he's searching for flaming diamonds again," said Mrs Morris. "As if that hasn't caused enough bother already. Now, stop that, Monkey Onassis, and come here at once."

"No, leave him, Ma," said Maisie. "I think he's onto something."

Monkey Onassis had jumped onto Lester's shoulder and was poking around in his macintosh.

"Get him off me!" said Lester. "Arrest him, Boggit – he's a jewel thief."

Monkey Onassis put his paw inside Lester's right pocket and found a packet of stale mints, a paper clip and a betting slip for a horse called Tricky Dicky, but no diamond.

He looked in the other pocket but only found a greasy comb and a bottle of indigestion tablets but no diamond.

But then he poked his paw into Lester's inside pocket. His face lit up. Because when he pulled his paw out, clenched in his hairy fist was something very sparkly indeed.

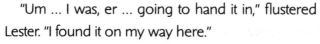

"Well, well, well," said PC Boggit. "What have we here then?"

"The diamond eggcup!" said Maisie.

"Um ... I was, er ... going to hand it in," flustered Lester. "I found it on my way here."

"A likely story," said PC Boggit.

"I ... er..." stammered Lester. But he didn't know what to say. He had been well and truly snared in his own big web of lies.

PC Boggit, however, knew exactly what to say.

"Lester Sylvester, I am arresting you for being a downright dirty liar, for falsifying newspaper stories and perverting the course of justice and getting innocent biscuit-makers, grumpy old men and monkeys into bother. And worst of all for nearly squishing Maisie Morris in a very messy manner. You do not have to say anything but anything you do say will be completely disregarded because it is probably another load of hogwash."

"Lordy me," said Old Soames. "I don't think anything so exciting has happened here since we changed over from steam to electrickery. I shall need a hot cup of cocoa to calm me nerves."

"And a nice jammy dodger," said Preston.

"Rot your teeth, they will," said Norman disapprovingly. But secretly, even he fancied a biscuit after everything that had happened.

"Wait a minute!" said Maisie. "There's one more thing to do. The *Chronicle* needs a new front page for tomorrow!"

"By golly!" said Ramsey. "The girl's right."

"Well, why don't you write it, Maisie?" said PC Boggit.

"Me?" said Maisie.

"Of course," said PC Boggit. "Then we'll know it's the truth."

"A splendid idea," said Ramsey. "You can type it up on my compooter when we get home."

Maisie smiled. She had done it. She had saved Norman Armour and Preston Braithwaite, she had saved Monkey Onassis, and what's more, she had saved her reputation.

The Truth

"LESTER THE LIAR," said the quadruple-height jumbo-sized capital letters on the front page of the *Chronicle* the next morning.

"Gosh," said Maisie as she read the copy over her bowl of Krispy Korny Flakes the next morning. "I still can't believe I wrote this!"

"Och, I can," said Ramsey. "It's wonderful."

"It is super, Maisie," added Mrs Morris. "But what about that newsflash at the bottom? Where did that come from?"

"BRUTON THE BULLY!" read Ramsey. *"Ms Norma Bruton, 47, a teacher at St Regina's Primary School, was sensationally sacked today after revelations that she had been locking her pupils in cupboards with no lunch. Further evidence, including a wet slipper and a pair of handcuffs, was uncovered in her big black leather bag."*

"Maisie, did you write this?" asked Mrs Morris.

"I don't know what you mean," said Maisie, and she looked at Ramsey and gave him a wink.

Ramsey smiled. "Well done, Maisie," he said. "You'll make a first-rate detective one day. I'm proud to have worked with you."

"Thanks," said Maisie, smiling. "But I think I'd rather be a journalist."

Ramsey laughed. "You know what?" he said. "I'll be glad when all the papers have to report is jam-making contests and novelty giant vegetables again. I think I preferred Groutley the way it was – small and dull!"

"Some hope with that monkey up to his tricks again," said Mrs Morris. "I don't think 'dull' is in his dictionary."

At that very moment Monkey Onassis was busy eating a boiled egg and soldiers out of his diamond-encrusted eggcup.

"I hope you're going to return that contraption later," added Mrs Morris.

"Oh yes," said Maisie. "And we're going to collect his reward."

"Yes, well, he won't be getting anything if it's all

covered in eggy crumbs, I'll warrant. And that reminds me, PC Boggit rang for you earlier. He said he's found out what sort of monkey Monkey Onassis is. Apparently he ran some tests when he was arrested."

"Oooh, what is he?" asked Maisie. "Sooty Mangabey? Buffy-headed Marmoset? Lesser Mouse Monkey?

"No," said Mrs Morris. "He says he's a Common Brown."

Maisie smiled at Monkey Onassis. "That must be a lie," she whispered. "There's nothing common about you whatsoever." And she hugged him so hard he dropped the diamond-encrusted eggcup onto the floor, where it spun for a second before rolling slowly along the lino and dropping down a crack under the cooker with a loud plop.

"Oops," said Maisie.

Epilogue

"Did I ever tell you about the time I nearly rescued the film star Sean McConnery?" asked Ramsey, perched on the edge of Maisie's bed, late one evening.

Maisie shook her head.

"Och, it's a famous tale," said Ramsey. "Full of intrigue and cunning and with a fearless hero with a wild ginger beard." And he winked at Maisie.

Maisie smiled and hugged Monkey Onassis tightly as Ramsey began his story.

But as Ramsey talked into the night in his soft Scottish lilt, Maisie's mind began to wander and she thought about everything that had happened that fateful week in Groutley.

Lester Sylvester was sentenced to ten years in the top-security prison, Groutley Scrubs.

He sits alone in his small cell, smoking nasty thin cigarettes and remembering how he was outwitted by an eight-year-old girl and a monkey.

Worst of all is the new prison governor who stalks the corridors whispering mean things through the iron bars and who rules the cell block with a rod of iron and a very, very long list of rules.

Ms Bruton found a new job after she was sacked from St Regina's. One where she can bully to her heart's content. And, of course, the inmates never dare to question her – or their punishment will be even longer in jail with her!

Norman Armour started a whole new chapter in his Misdemeanour Book devoted entirely to Monkey Onassis. He regularly writes to the Chronicle to complain about the monkey putting his feet on the bus seats and playing his kazoo too loudly in the Municipal Rose Gardens.

Maisie's class got a new, young and dynamic teacher called Bodmin Garfunkel, who keeps stick insects in a jar, wears stripy tank tops and lets the children call him Bod, much to Mrs Morris's disapproval.

PC Boggit went back to watching *Cops in Socks* and eating jam doughnuts. And Groutley got itself a second, part-time policeman: a tall, gangly, ginger fellow with a nose for a mystery – Ramsey McDoon.

Monkey Onassis did not go back to school but kept up to his awful tricks by removing the bottom eight steps of the main staircase at Withering Heights, stranding everyone on the first floor for a whole day.

Preston Braithwaite gave Maisie a year's supply of coconut snowballs to thank her for rescuing him, which Monkey Onassis managed to eat in one day, making himself very sick – all over Mrs Morris's new raffia rug.

What about Belinda? Did she stop bullying? Did she and Maisie become friends?

Not a chance. She and Lindy and Mindy were as

mean and rotten to Maisie as ever. But Maisie didn't care, because she had the best friends in the world – Monkey Onassis and Ramsey McDoon.

"And so you see, Maisie," continued Ramsey, still on his story of the kidnapped film star, "there's never any need to lie, because the truth is so often stranger than fiction."

But Maisie didn't hear him. She was fast asleep.

Maisie Morris lives with her mum in a titchy turret at the top of Withering Heights Retirement Home. While Mrs Morris looks after the residents, polishing bottoms and scrubbing smalls, Maisie plays cards and learns how to quickstep with the flamboyant Loveday Pink.

But they all live in fear of the odious owners, Mr and Mrs Arkwright, who serve cabbage water for lunch, confiscate pets and cancel Christmas. Maisie is convinced that nothing less than a miracle will deal with the revolting pair.

The great thing about miracles, though, is that you never know when one is lurking round the corner...

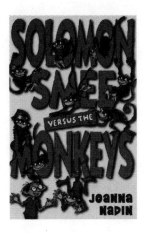

In the Kingdom of Elsewhere, just to the left of
Nomansland and not far from Xanadu, sits Royal
Nerdal Norton – a town so small and insignificant
that only the gods and mapmakers have heard of it.
And now you, of course.

The town of Royal Nerdal Norton has a problem.
Small brown monkeys are causing all manner of
mischief and bother, and not even Maurice Hankey,
the incompetent court magician, or Terry Bunce, the
haphazard inventor, can help. So it's up to Solomon
Smee, a small boy with brown-rimmed glasses and
dark, dark hair, to save the day!

Get in the Judy Moody mood!

Bad moods, good moods, even back-to-school moods – Judy has them all! But when her new teacher gives the class a "Me" collage project, Judy has so much fun she nearly forgets to be moody!

Meet Judy, her little "bother" Stink, her best friend Rocky and her "pest" friend Frank Pearl. They're sure to put you in a very Judy Moody mood!

When she was ten years old, Katrina Picket woke
Merlin. It was quite by accident – she'd had no
intention of doing any such thing. But it was
fortunate for everyone in England that she did. They
didn't know, of course. The whole thing had to be
hushed up. Most people thought it was a particularly
inventive party for the Queen's jubilee. And as for
the dragon and the exploding fireball – they were
explained away as impressive special effects.

But Katrina, and the Prime Minister, knew different...

It's Pony Day at Merryfield Hall Riding School and, for the first time ever, Dad has promised to come and watch Amber jump. Everything will be perfect ... as long as Amber gets to ride her favourite pony, Beany. But Donna wants to ride Beany too – and, as the jumping competition gets closer, it looks like she'll go to any lengths to get her own way!